The Diamond Horse

Stacy Gregg
The Diamond Horse

HarperCollins *Children's Books*

First published in Great Britain by HarperCollins *Children's Books* 2016
Published in this edition 2017
HarperCollins *Children's Books* is a division of HarperCollins*Publishers* Ltd
1 London Bridge Street
London SE1 9GH

The HarperCollins website address is
www.harpercollins.co.uk
1

ISBN: 978–0–00–812440–3

Typeset by Palimpsest Book Production Limited, Falkirk, Stirlingshire

Printed and bound in England by
Clays, Ltd, St Ives plc

MIX
Paper from
responsible sources
FSC™ C007454

FSC™ is a non-profit international organisation established to promote
the responsible management of the world's forests. Products carrying the
FSC label are independently certified to assure consumers that they come
from forests that are managed to meet the social, economic and
ecological needs of present and future generations,
and other controlled sources.

Find out more about HarperCollins and the environment at
www.harpercollins.co.uk/green

For Celeste

Prologue

As the blizzard closed in, Anna Orlov struggled to make out the lights of the palace on the horizon. Their starry shimmer had been the beacon guiding her home, but as their glow became obscured by the snowstorm Anna felt as if she was fading too. Submerged deep beneath the snowdrifts, her feet had long ago turned numb, and her heavy skirts, soaked through and stiff with ice, threatened to drag her down with every step.

Yet it was not her own failing strength that worried her most. It was Drakon. The race across the taiga had left her horse ragged with exhaustion, and the wound on his shoulder had opened into a raw slash of crimson that seeped into his silver dapples. As he stumbled alongside her in the deep snow, Anna's heart was breaking. With every step she could hear the dark rasp of his mighty lungs, his wide fluted nostrils misting hot plumes into the frozen air.

Dragon's breath. That was how it looked. And hadn't Drakon always reminded her of a dragon? Something about the shape of his head, that great, solid slab of his mighty jawbone, the way it narrowed to the slender taper of his fine muzzle. With enormous Asiatic eyes, dark and intense, trimmed with long lashes, his features would have been better suited to a dragon. That was how he had been given his name.

The rest of Drakon was no less peculiar. His body was out of all proportion for he had been born with an extra rib, which elongated his physique, making him as lean and sleek as a racing hound. He was all muscle and sinew, with a dapple-grey coat strung over a bony frame. His legs, buried deep in the snowdrifts, were so long they looked like they belonged to another creature entirely. They gave him his power, made him swift and sure-footed across the treacherous black ice of the frozen rivers.

Drakon's strides had pounded out a relentless drumbeat across the Russian taiga, but their cadence had weakened until now it had become a desperate struggle to place one hoof in front of the other.

"Come on! It is not much further," Anna promised her horse. But in reality, she had no idea how far away the palace was, or even if it was ahead of them at all. There was nothing to guide her any more. Just the snow and the darkness, her numb feet and ice-bitten cheeks, singing with the pain of air so cold it pierced her brain.

"We must keep moving, Drakon..."

With his head hanging low, the horse managed to take another step, then suddenly he lurched sideways, his legs buckling beneath him.

"Drakon!"

Anna flung herself at him, clinging to his neck. Her fur-gloved fingers twisted into the rope of the stallion's silvery mane. "Drakon, please! Please..."

Drakon was a dead weight plummeting, his magnificent swan neck twisting and jerking as he went down. Anna gasped as she felt the sting of the snow flung up in his wake like an ocean wave striking a ship's bow.

Shocked by the fall, the horse instinctively tried to get back to his feet, forelegs twitching as he struggled, swinging his neck to raise his head. Then, with a pitiful groan, he gave in to exhaustion and collapsed back into the icy drifts.

"*Niet!*" Anna's hands grabbed at him, tearing his mane as she tried to drag him to his feet once more. "*Niet*! Drakon! Get up!"

It was no good. How could she possibly lift the horse when she had barely enough strength to hold herself upright?

Anna straightened up, panting from the effort of trying to raise Drakon, and looked around. The blizzard swirled about her and she couldn't see a thing. She had no idea what direction the palace might be in. Even if she could make it home and raise a search party, how would they ever find Drakon out here in the snow? Already his silver dapples were barely visible against the drifts, and the white powder kept steadily falling, so that soon it would blanket and disguise him completely.

Niet. It was hopeless.

Anna's gloved hands fumbled to loosen the belt on her thick sable fur coat. She already felt frozen to the bone, but as the fur fell away from her bare shoulders and the last remnants of body heat were stolen she realised there were greater pains to endure. Beneath the fur she had worn her grey satin gown, corseted so tight at the waist it made her slight twelve-year-old physique appear even more fragile and birdlike. Her skin was the palest alabaster and she looked almost translucent against the snow as she dropped to her knees next to Drakon. With trembling hands, she draped her coat so that it covered the chest and shoulders of her horse.

"It's just like the old days, Drakon. Riding in the woods…" Anna murmured as she arranged the fur and then manoeuvred herself beneath it so that she was nestled into the crook of her horse's forelimbs, tucked up against his ribcage.

"Remember how we slept underneath the stars? With the rugs laid beneath us and Vasily tending the fire pit to heat his urn of spiced honey tea, and

Igor whimpering as he dreamt of chasing timber wolves…"

She whispered on to her horse and tugged the fur coat up to her chest. As she did this, her gloved fingertips brushed against the chain round her neck. The necklace was still there. After all they had been through, it was a miracle that it had not been lost.

With frozen hands she clasped the stone and repeated the ritual that had comforted her ever since she had been ten years old. Ever since the fateful day that her mother had placed the precious gift round her daughter's neck.

Anna raised the black gem up to her face, holding it close so that she could gaze upon its dark beauty as her mother's words came back to her:

"Never seek to understand its power. And do not try to control it. Past and present and future all lie within this necklace, but it is the stone that decides what you will see."

Anna gazed deep into the diamond. The brilliant cut refracted and reflected her vision, splintering the world into a million tiny pieces, as infinite as the snowflakes that flurried around her. Then the stars turned dark and she saw the amber glint of a tiger's eye, the flash of his stripes and the low rumble of his growl.

Instinctively, Anna clutched her hands to her throat and the diamond slipped from her fingers. Then, with her skin as pale and cold as the snow that surrounded her, she fell back at last against her beloved horse.

CHAPTER 1

The Snow Palace of Count Orlov

Three years earlier...

Anna ran through the palace corridors, her breath coming in quick, painful gasps, her heart pounding. Behind her, the rumbling growl of the wolfhound became more menacing as he grew nearer, closing in on her with every stride.

"*Niet!* Please! Stop!"

The marble floors were slippery beneath her feet and as she rounded the corner by the grand ballroom, Anna found herself sliding out of control. Her shoulder glanced hard into the corner of a gigantic oil painting of her father, Count Orlov, mounted on horseback and brandishing a sabre, and tilted it dangerously to one side.

The hound lost his balance on the corner too. As she pelted away, Anna heard the thin screech of his claws as he scrambled frantically to get a foothold, paws skidding across the glassy surface. Then he was up and running again, gaining on her once more. Anna threw a look back over her shoulder and the choking pain in her chest made it impossible to run any more.

She was simply laughing too hard.

She collapsed forward, her hands on her knees, trying to catch her breath and giggling madly. "Wait, Igor…"

The puppy did not stop. Delighted to have bested her, he made a dramatic leap into the air and came crashing down on top of his mistress.

"Igor!" Anna shrieked as she went down in a heap on the floor, the skirts of her silk gown entangling them both. She rolled on to her back with the borzoi on top of her. Igor was still play-growling and refusing to give up the game, making darting lunges at her face as she fended him off.

"Igor, *niet!*" Anna grappled the snarling bundle of fluff out from the folds of her gown and held him aloft in both hands so that he was dangling above her. Suspended in mid-air, Igor wriggled and squirmed, his little legs waving about wildly, his mouth wide open in a toothy grin. "You are so fearsome!" Anna teased him. "Oh, but I am terrified of you, such a big powerful wolfhound you are, Igor!"

Igor swooped down and his pink, wet tongue slushed over Anna's cheek. "Ick! Doggy breath!" She screwed up her face in revulsion. "Come on, Igor! Be a good borzoi now!"

Borzoi – the word meant "swift". Anna's father, Count Orlov, had given this name to his hounds because, as he often boasted, "they are the fastest in all of Russia".

In the royal court of Empress Catherine they praised Count Orlov as an "alchemist of nature". He was a magician, the master of the dark art of manipulating bloodlines to create strange and fantastical new beasts.

To Anna, who had grown up at Khrenovsky, their palace estate, surrounded by her father's "living experiments", it seemed commonplace to share her home with a menagerie of rare and exotic animals.

It felt perfectly natural that a pair of Amur leopards in black velvet collars roamed the palace halls, although Katia, the head of housekeeping, was less than impressed when they clambered all over the velvet *chaise longues* in the drawing room. The cooks too, were not so happy that a family of cheeky long-tailed squirrels had taken up residence in the kitchen and would leave half-gnawed loaves of bread and nibbled apples in their wake.

Count Orlov gave the animals free rein and no room in the palace was sacred. The chandeliers in the grand ballroom were alive with the beating wings of the butterflies who clustered around the crystals. Pythons lazed in the bathtubs and refused to budge. When Anna entered the drawing room for breakfast the air would be filled with green-throated parakeets, thrashing the air with vermilion wings.

There were a few creatures that the Count considered too large or too wild to dwell inside the palace walls, and these were housed outdoors. Leading away from the grand western entrance of the palace there was a winding maze of topiary that led across the lawns to a series of elaborate gilt cages. Row upon row of these golden prisons housed animals gathered from all over Russia and the lands beyond. Two enormous Siberian bears, captured to be a mating pair, occupied one of the largest cages. Anna thought them a sadly ill-suited couple. The male was much older and more careworn than his mate, with a tattered coat and chunks ripped from his ears. He had a permanent scowl on his face and lumbered about his cage as if he was always spoiling for a fight. The female was much smaller and younger, and had glorious rich, dark brown fur. Her muzzle wrinkled when she growled, giving her a sweet expression, and her dark cherry eyes stared wistfully out through the bars, as if she were desperate to escape both captivity and her arranged marriage.

In the golden cage beside the bears, silver foxes made themselves invisible during the day. Lurking underground in their burrow, they would emerge at nightfall to snap and snarl at each other over chopped-up chunks of meat that Anna had tossed into their cage, crunching the bones with their pointed canines.

The beautiful musk deer who lived in the cage next door would shrink back as the foxes growled over their supper. Wide-eyed, with soft taupe fur, they seemed the most gentle of all the creatures in the menagerie, but they had needle teeth that protruded like vampires' fangs from their velvet muzzles.

The deer did not bite, but the little minks who scurried about in their long, low cage were savage. Their teeth, tiny and white, were as sharp as knives. "You will lose your fingers if you are not careful," Vasily the groom would warn Anna when he found her stroking the baby minks through the grille of their cage.

Vasily came up from the stables once a day to fill the cages with straw. He was different from the rest of the serfs in Count Orlov's service. A head taller than any other man at the stables, he was broad-shouldered and strong. And while the other serfs had the appearance of boiled potatoes, Anna thought Vasily handsome, with his thick russet hair, high cheekbones and deep, brooding eyes.

Sullen and serious, Vasily did not smile easily, and Anna liked to set herself the challenge of making him laugh.

"I have taught the mink a new trick!" she would exclaim whenever he arrived with the straw for the cages. "Come and see!"

The mink were untameable and their "tricks" mostly involved standing on their hind legs and nipping food from Anna's fingers, which only made Vasily beg her to stop.

"They will not hurt me," Anna would laugh at him. She had no fear of any of the animals. Any… except the timber wolves. There was something in the way they glowered at her, shoulders hunched in menace as they paced the perimeter of their gilt cage, jaws hanging open, white teeth glistening. It was as if they were just waiting for the bars to part, biding their time until they could devour her.

Once, her brother Ivan had dared her to go inside their cage. She had refused at first, but Ivan was good at bullying her into doing things she shouldn't. He was three years older than Anna and in their lonely palace in the wilderness he was her only playmate.

"This is the game," he told her. "You walk in, and I will lock the gate behind you and then I count to ten and let you out again."

Anna looked at the wolves. They were pacing the bars, their hackles raised.

"I don't want to," she said.

"I knew you were a coward," Ivan said.

"I'm not a coward," Anna insisted.

"Then do it!"

Anna pushed the fear down into her belly and stepped closer to the cage.

Ivan kept goading her. "Pathetic baby sister!" he gloated. "You need to show them you are not afraid."

The wolf pack were waiting, pacing and watching her, glassy-eyed and panting, jaws open in anticipation. Anna didn't want to get any closer, but Ivan kept taunting her.

"Come on, open the door and get in the cage. What are you scared of? They will not bite…"

Anna stepped forward and shut her eyes tight as she stretched out her hand to grasp the cage door. She began to swing the door back and as she did so the largest wolf lunged for her. He threw himself at the bars of the gate, shoulder-barging it with his full weight, trying to force his way through. He would have succeeded, if it were not for the giant of a man who stepped between the girl and the wolf. He thrust the gate shut and yanked Anna fiercely by the shoulder so that she was thrown back out of danger.

Anna found herself sprawled on the ground, panting and looking up at her father, who towered over her like a monster. His face was crimson with rage, except for the thin white line of the scar that ran from his temple to his chin. *Le Balafre* – it was his nickname in the royal court, where they whispered it in French – Scarface.

"Idiot child! What were you thinking?"

"I wasn't… Ivan dared me to do it!" Anna blurted out the words and instantly regretted them. Her brother had ways of making her pay if she told on him.

Count Orlov turned to his son.

"It was a game," Ivan said airily. "We were only playing."

Many years later, Anna would look back on this moment and remember the sickening smile that had played on Ivan's lips when he spoke.

*

"He hates me," Anna complained to her mother, later that day.

Anna was sitting cross-legged on a velvet cushion, watching with total absorption as her mother, the Countess, arranged her potions in front of the mirror to begin her *toilette*.

"He doesn't hate you, Anna," the Countess replied, staring into the mirror and picking up a powder puff, buffing the powder into the alabaster skin of her *décolletage*. "He is envious, that is all. You have a way with animals, and a natural charm. Your brother on the other hand..." the Countess hesitated. "... Ivan is not so blessed as you."

Countess Orlov tapped her fingertip into a tiny

pot of rouge and sucked in her cheeks to dab it on, then used the same crimson stain to paint in the cupid's bow of her lips. With a kohl pencil, she defined the arch of her brows. Finally, with the very tip of the pencil, she added a black dot like a punctuation mark above her top lip.

"Why are you doing that?" Anna asked.

"It is the fashion in Versailles to have a beauty spot," the Countess replied. Her gaze fixed on Anna's eyes reflected in the mirror. "And the Empress likes anything that is French."

"Why does she want us to copy the French? We are Russians."

The Countess put down the kohl pencil and turned to her daughter. "But Empress Catherine is not true Russian, is she? Our Empress was born German. Yet she speaks French at court because that is the language of sophistication and culture."

Anna frowned. "Why don't we speak our own language?"

"Only serfs speak Russian," the Countess said. "This is why you must pay attention to your studies with Clarise."

Anna rolled her eyes at the mention of her tutor and the Countess cast her a stern look. "One day you will be old enough to join us for a dinner party like the one we are having tonight and then you will need your very best French, *oui?*"

"*Oui!*" Anna giggled. It was so nice to see her mother like this, dressed up so beautifully, her eyes shining at the prospect of glamorous company. Often at the Khrenovsky estate it felt as if they were in total isolation, so far away from the bustle of the city of Moscow and even further still from St Petersburg, where her father devoted himself to life at court in the service of the Empress.

Tonight's dinner was a farewell to her father who was about to depart once more for St Petersburg. The meal would be served in the grand dining room and all the nobles from the neighbouring estates had been invited. Anna had watched with fascination as endless bouquets of lily of the valley and white tulips were carried upstairs by the housemaids. Their sweet and sickly aroma now filled the bedchambers of the palace while downstairs tea roses in delicate shades of peach and cream tumbled out of ivy-clad urns.

In the grand marble hallways, young serving boys with rags tied to the soles of their feet swept through the halls as if they were ice-skating, using their gliding movements to buff the floors until they gleamed.

A hunting party had been sent out the day before and had returned with wild boar and deer. In the kitchens the cooks set about preparing the meat, pots and pans banging and fires roaring as they busily chopped beetroots and scoured potatoes for the banquet.

The peacocks, who often roamed the corridors, had been banished outdoors by Katia, the head maid, because they made too much mess. But the Amur leopards still had the run of the place and presently they were lounging on the Countess's bed as Anna stroked their velvety fur.

The Countess lifted up a silver powdered wig and swept back her luxurious blonde hair under the elaborately stacked hairpiece.

"What do you think, *milochka*?" She poked at the wig, repositioning it on top of her beautiful blonde tresses. "Do I look pretty?"

"It's grey, Mama," Anna replied. "It makes you look old."

The Countess's smile disappeared for a moment but then she regained her composure. "Powdered wigs are very Parisian. You do not understand fashion yet, my little one," she said sweetly.

From a dark blue box on the dressing table the Countess picked out a pair of black diamond earrings, their tiered crystals glistening like miniature chandeliers. She put aside the earrings and then picked up the box that had been stacked beneath.

Anna's heart leapt. She rose from her velvet cushion and came over to stand at her mother's shoulder.

"Can I open it for you?"

The Countess smiled. "Of course."

Inside, nestled against silver silk, was a priceless necklace. The black diamond, attached to a silver filigree chain, draped across the cloth like a glittering teardrop, the size of a walnut. Round the brilliant-cut gemstone a setting of smaller, white diamonds created a halo that contrasted its rare dark beauty.

"It is so beautiful," Anna breathed. "Where did it come from?"

She had heard this story a million times, but she still wanted to hear it once more.

"It was given to me by my mother," the Countess said. "And to her by my grandmother. It is a family heirloom, passed down from generation to generation. One day, *milochka*, I will give it to you."

The Countess fixed the clasp on her earrings and looked at herself admiringly in the mirror. Then she reached out her milk-white fingers to grasp the silver chain and lift the necklace from its case. She was about to lift it up when there was a knock at the door.

"Come in," called Anna's mother.

"Excuse me, Countess?" Katia, the head maid, quietly entered the bedchamber.

"Yes, Katia? What is it?"

"There is a problem in the dining room. We have Count Tolstoy seated next to Count Bobrinsky…"

The Countess stood up. "That will not do at all! They cannot stand each other!" She made her way briskly to the door. "You had better show me what can be done. Quickly now, Katia!"

And with that, the two women left the room.

Anna waited until their footsteps had receded down the corridor and then she sat herself down at the Countess's dressing table.

She twisted up her dark blonde hair and secured it in a loose bun on top of her head, revealing the pale ivory skin beneath, just like her mother's.

As the diamond teardrop fell against her breastbone, Anna admired its darkness. It contrasted against the whiteness of her skin, the light glowing from inside the stone as if it were on fire. For a moment she was lost in its beauty, and then she raised her eyes to see her reflection. But the eyes that returned Anna's gaze were not her own. There was a girl looking back at her from the mirror who Anna had never seen before.

The girl in the mirror was blonde too, her ice-white hair twisted in a braid on top of her head, her alabaster skin glimmering as if it had been dusted with stars. She wore a glittering costume that shone like a star, covered with silver spangles. She was leaning into the mirror and painting on make-up, lining her lips with a brilliant scarlet.

Anna stared at the girl. And, holding Anna's gaze, the girl in the mirror smiled right back at her! Then she smacked her red lips together and adjusted her glittering costume, wriggling the straps so that her silver spangles shimmied. Then the ice-white blonde reached out to the dresser in front of her and lifted a black diamond necklace to her throat. It was identical to Anna's. They were both wearing the same necklace!

Anna reached out her hand to the mirror glass. The girl smiled again and then she stood up. There were voices in the distance calling out her name:

Valentina, Valentina, it is time…

Chapter 2

The Moscow Spectacular

In the wings behind the velvet curtains, Valentina Romanov was dashing up the rungs of the rope ladder. Through the curtains she could see the spotlights beginning to circle, seeking her out. The drums were rolling.

When she reached the platform at the very peak of the big top, Valentina rose to her feet and stood curling her toes over the edge before looking down. She was twenty metres above the ground with nothing to hold on to and no safety net. Below her she could see the tigers prowling out of the ring, their shoulders hunched as if in a sulk, their performance over for the evening. Now, it was her turn.

The music swelled and the spotlights swooped up to expose her to the audience at last. Valentina struck a pose: one hand raised in a flourish above her head, the other grasping the wooden bar of the trapeze. And then, without hesitation, she leapt.

She flew out into mid-air and then felt the jerk of the trapeze snatching her back again. The spotlight followed Valentina as she swung back and forth like a pendulum. When she reached the highest point of her arc she suddenly let go of the wooden bar. She twisted her whole body high in the air so that her hands now gripped the bar facing the other way. Then, with her elbows locked into position, she executed a half-pike, turning and flipping her knees over the bar to dangle upside down.

As she felt the blood rush to her head the music changed to a familiar tune that signalled the arrival of the clowns.

Valentina could never figure out why people liked clowns. She found their white greasepaint faces and gigantic red lipstick smiles disturbing. What was funny about the way they charged around like idiots, pushing each other and falling over their own feet?

Yet their antics instantly brought on gales of laughter from the audience. The clowns ran into the ring below her, leaping up on top of each other's shoulders to make a human pyramid, juggling batons and knocking each other off stilts, and all the while Valentina swung high above them, waiting for her moment.

The spotlights suddenly flew skywards and Valentina grasped the bar and performed a double-flip, pushing up so that she was almost doing a handstand. She twisted round and round, somersaulting in mid-air, and on the third twist her hands suddenly slipped loose from the bar.

There was a horrified gasp from the crowd. Valentina looked down as the ground came hurtling up to meet her and automatically braced, going into a tumble roll. In the ring below, the clowns sprang into position, forming a circle and pulling the firemen's net taut between them.

She landed smack in the centre, curling like a ball on impact and rebounding up into the air. As she flew upwards she did a knee tuck like a diver on a high board, and then, with an easy grace, she reached up to grasp the red silk sash dangling from the rooftop.

The crowd, now realising the fall had been a part of the act, began to clap enthusiastically. Valentina wrapped herself in the sash and started to twirl, rotating one way and then the other, unwinding like a spinning top. She did the splits, throwing her head back and arching her spine, as if being held by an invisible tango partner. The silver spangles on her costume sparkled like a mirror ball in the spotlight and then, in a flash, there were three more spotlights, their beams illuminating the ring below. The clowns had disappeared and the lights traced patterns on the empty space. The drumroll quickened, the lights circled faster and then the velvet curtains were flung to one side as Sasha made his grand entrance.

So far tonight the audience had witnessed a snarling ambush of golden tigers, a bear on a unicycle, and monkeys in waistcoats and top hats riding dogs in tutus. All the same, when a pink horse came cantering into the ring, they truly thought their eyes were deceiving them. Surely the strange colour must have been a trick of the light? But as the spotlights cast their beam on the horse it became clear that he really was pink – the softest, most delicate shade of rose, with a silvery mane and tail.

Despite his pretty colour, Sasha was clearly a stallion, with a heavy crested neck, broad chest and powerful shoulders. Standing at almost seventeen hands, he seemed even taller due to the silver plume he wore that stood straight up in a stiff crown between his ears. On his back he wore a matching silver saddle blanket, surcingled round his belly with two vaulting handles attached on either side of his withers.

The extraordinary horse cantered straight into the ring and immediately settled into a big loping stride, circling the perimeter. Above him, Valentina began to swing from the red silk sash in circles matching the circuits of the horse below, manoeuvring herself into position. Then she let go once more and plummeted down.

She landed on Sasha's back with feline grace, gripped the handles on the vaulting pad and pushed herself into a handstand. She held the pose for an entire lap of the ring as the crowd applauded loudly. Then she dropped back down, put her feet on Sasha's rump and straightened up, so that she was standing on the hindquarters of the horse as he continued his steady canter.

With a backward flip Valentina dismounted and did two brisk cartwheels, bounding across the sand to meet Sasha on the other side of the ring and vault back up again. This time she swung herself up into the saddle so that she was sitting back to front, facing his tail. She stood up with her hands above her head and leapt into the air, doing sideways splits before landing with her feet on the horse's broad rump and sliding down his tail to hit the ground running.

The crowd were cheering her on, and with every backflip and somersault Valentina and Sasha won them over.

As the pink horse reared up on his hind legs and pirouetted in a circle as if he were dancing in time with the music the big top audience went wild with applause. Valentina leapt down to take a bow and the audience roared with delighted laughter as

Sasha nodded and then bowed beside her, dropping down to his knees, one foreleg outstretched, head lowered in reverence. Then the horse and the girl were on their feet again, Valentina smiling and waving goodbye as they ran from the ring and into the wings.

"Valentina!" Sergei the ringmaster was waiting for her. It had been a pitch-perfect performance tonight – their act had been utterly faultless.

She smiled at the ringmaster. "Yes, Sergei?"

"There is elephant dung by the caravans," Sergei said. "Clean it up before you feed the tigers."

Valentina felt her cheeks flush pink with shame. Had she really been stupid enough to think he was going to praise her? The ringmaster never had a kind word for anyone, least of all his star trapeze artist and her pink horse.

Sergei was a tiny man, short and squat, not much bigger than the circus dwarves, with a downturned grouper mouth and pale rheumy eyes. He had been Valentina's guardian ever since her mother died.

"I could have left you on the orphanage steps," he liked to remind her. "A snot-nosed gypsy girl like you should be grateful I gave her such a home."

Three performances a day including matinees: that was the price of Valentina's "home" at the Moscow Spectacular. For this she received no pay, but she had bed and board in a dilapidated caravan that she shared with the contortionist, Irina. She had nothing in the world of her own. No clothes apart from her leotards and a dirty old tracksuit that she wore while she cleaned out the animal trailers. No toys and no dolls and no books. She had never been taught to read or add or subtract. Valentina was not allowed to go to school.

"A circus is never in one place long enough," Sergei had dismissed her pleas. "Besides, a girl like you has no need for education."

Valentina knew nothing about art, history or the countries of the world. She wouldn't even have been able to locate Moscow on a map. She was thirteen and she could barely scrawl her own name.

And yet her talent and abilities shone as bright as the spangled costumes she wore for her performances. She had a photographic memory and would only need to run through a routine once before it was imprinted in her mind so that she would never forget it. Compared to the other circus kids – Irina the contortionist, or Magda the fortune-teller's brood of sallow-skinned, dark-eyed children, the lantern-jawed offspring of the strong man and his fierce red-faced wife – Valentina stood out as clever, brave and resilient, able to tumble from the trapeze to the nets and bounce back up again with a smile on her face. But it was her way with the animals that truly marked Valentina out as unique. She would sit for hours and watch the circus beasts in their cages. She could read their moods so well that before she was even ten years old she was being trusted to care for the tigers by herself. While the other performers shrank back in fear of their snarling jaws and razor-sharp talons, Valentina thought nothing of taking hefty, meaty bones and thrusting them through the cage bars. Her favourite tiger, Mischa, would even take meat straight from her hand, though she rarely fed him like this when Sergei was watching.

"You are no good to me without hands!" he would admonish without any humour. It was never too late to be dropped off at the orphanage, according to Sergei.

The tigers padded up to the bars of their cages and smooched and preened like pussycats whenever she came near, and it was clear to Valentina that they would never harm her. All the animals in the circus adored her, but it was Sasha alone that she truly loved. She had known the horse all her life.

He had been an ungainly-looking colt, with a huge head attached to a long neck, and an even longer body, legs like a giraffe and great slabs of knees and dinner-plate hooves. But when he began to move, there was something completely mesmerising about him. He was trainable too. Valentina had taught him to bow by taking a carrot and passing it down between his forelegs until Sasha dropped to his knees and lowered his head to reach the tasty treat. It had taken him one day to master this.

By the time he was three, Valentina's stallion had been able to rear and pirouette on cue. Soon, it was Sasha and Valentina whose faces appeared on the circus posters. Sergei understood the allure of the tiny blonde girl and her gigantic pink horse, and he made them his headline act.

"The stars of the circus," Valentina murmured as she led Sasha back to his tiny yard. "How lucky we are." The pink horse shook out his mane and blew through his wide nostrils as if in agreement.

Valentina had a long night ahead of her feeding the other animals and cleaning out the trailers, but first she took care of Sasha. She mucked out his yard, gave him fresh hay and refilled his water. Then she mixed his feed, oats and chaff and barley, giving the horse twice as much as Sergei permitted. The ringmaster kept all the animals on starvation rations to save money. "Your horse eats my profits!" he would often tell Valentina. "And still its ribs stick out."

Valentina hated the way Sergei spoke of the animals as if they were nothing more than props for his circus performances. She did the best she could to protect Sasha and the others, to make their miserable lives better than they were. Sometimes, when she saw the shackles on the elephant's ankles, or the frustration on the faces of the poor monkeys cooped up in their tiny cages all day, she found herself weeping.

"You are too soft. They are just animals," Irina would say when she found Valentina in their caravan, her cheeks wet with tears.

A scrawny waif with hollow eyes and grey skin, Irina had the rare ability to be double-jointed in both her elbows and knees, which made her a brilliant contortionist. She had been ten years old when she ran away from the orphanage to join the Moscow Spectacular.

"I have fallen on my feet here," Irina would often say. It was an ironic turn of phrase because in fact Irina never fell on her feet – she usually fell on her backside. This was why Sergei would not let her even be Valentina's understudy on the high wire. The girl had no poise or balance, so that even the clowns held their breath with concern every time she went up the trapeze.

Sergei had put Irina in Valentina's caravan and they soon became best friends. Irina, however, was not an easy room-mate. Valentina would often find her practising her contortionist's tricks, curled up like a pretzel on the floor, or walking on her hands and using her feet to make a cup of gypsy tea. At night they slept in twin beds side by side and Valentina would often be woken by Irina whimpering in her sleep. The whimpers would grow more intense until their caravan echoed with Irina's sobs, growing louder and more panic-stricken until suddenly the girl would sit bolt upright and start screaming. Then Valentina would hurry over to her friend's bedside and hug her, rocking her from side to side until her night terrors subsided.

Once, after a particularly bad episode, Valentina had asked her friend what it was that she dreamt about that was so frightening.

"Oh, but it is not a dream!" Irina said. "That is the problem, don't you see? I am not dreaming. I am *remembering*. In my mind I am back at the orphanage. I can smell the stench of the babies in their dirty nappies. I hear the hungry cries of the other children and I see the sickly ones lying in their cots alongside me. That is when I wake up and thank God that I escaped and found my way here."

Irina thought the circus was the best place in the

world and never understood Valentina's urge to run away from it.

One night, Valentina had shown Irina the sheet of paper that she kept hidden beneath the loose floorboard in their caravan. On it there was a picture of a horse, a very beautiful creature being ridden in a grand arena. The rider wore a top hat and tails, and the horse had its mane braided. Beneath the image there was writing.

"What does it say?" Irina asked.

Valentina could not read the words but she knew what the sheet of paper said – she had memorised it long ago. "It is the application form for the Federation Dressage Academy," she said. "This is the greatest dressage school in the whole of Russia. The Olympic team train here. This is where Sasha and I are going to go."

Irina looked at her, totally baffled. "But you do not ride dressage! You are circus!"

Valentina shrugged. "I taught Sasha how to stand on his hind legs and dance; how much harder can these dressage tricks be?"

"Sergei would never let you go," Irina looked

worried. "Oh, Valentina, please do not have such dreams! They will only disappoint you."

Valentina loved Irina and felt terribly sad that the fear of ending up back in the orphanage was enough to keep the girl at the circus. Sergei's clever manipulations meant Irina had lost all hope of any other kind of life. And Valentina could not persuade her friend to think otherwise. When the time to leave came, it would be only her and Sasha, and she dared not tell anyone else.

That night when Valentina got back from cleaning up the tigers' cages Irina was already asleep. She snored loudly, snuffling and wheezing like an old man. Valentina worked quietly, so that her roommate would not waken, as she jimmied up the floorboard beside her bed and pulled out the treasured piece of paper. She traced her fingers over the words, remembering how her mother had read them out to her, with Valentina on her knee.

"This is your destiny, *milochka*," she had told her daughter. "You will have a big life, a grand life! You will go to places and see things that will astound you. You cannot even imagine the world that is out there waiting for you, Valentina. You are going to be a superstar far greater than this circus has ever seen."

Valentina put her hand beneath the floorboards once more and this time she lifted out a velvet bag with a tasselled drawstring. Inside was the only other memento she had of her mother, the gift she had given her before she died. Apart from Sasha, the contents of this bag meant more to her than anything else in the world.

In the dim light of her bedside lamp, Valentina sat down on her bed, clasping the velvet bag to her chest. On the wall by her pillow she had hung a small mirror, slightly cracked in one corner. She looked at her reflection and saw a dirty, unloved circus girl. Then, from the velvet bag she withdrew the necklace. She raised her hands behind her neck and fastened the silver filigree clasp so that the black teardrop-shaped stone fell at her throat. In the cracked mirror, the magnificent necklace sparkled brightly, and Valentina was suddenly in a giant stadium. There were thousands of people rising to their feet, applauding, and Sasha danced beneath her, glorious and perfect as he trotted to the music.

Valentina knew in that moment that this was no a dream. It was real and true, and all she had to do was make a leap of faith. Throw herself into the air and forget the safety net. Somehow, she would make it happen.

CHAPTER 3

Black Diamond

The arrival of two Siberian tigers at the Khrenovsky estate was the talk of the palace and the entire staff gathered on the lawn to greet the new additions to Count Orlov's menagerie.

Anna stood beside Katia as the tigers arrived in a steel-barred crate on a carriage towed by eight horses. Three times the size of the Amur leopards, the striped beasts swiped their paws menacingly at the assembled crowd and let loose growls that sent the younger maids running and shrieking across the lawn. The servant boys fell back from the cage in terror too. Only Vasily kept calm, walking right past the snarling beasts to unharness the carriage horses.

The horses had been rendered rake-thin and exhausted by their long journey. "Poor things." Vasily shook his head in dismay. "How gruelling it must have been to hear the constant, inescapable growl of tigers at their heels no matter how fast they ran... It must have driven them mad."

"They will be all right, won't they?" Anna asked.

Vasily looked even more serious than usual. "I will do my best for them, Lady Anna," was all he said. While Vasily led the weakened carriage horses away to the stables the serfs pondered the problem of how to unload the tigers without getting near them. Eventually they decided to use wooden poles, passed through the steel-barred crate so that ten men on either side could lift it in unison. They would then carry the steel crate and the tigers inside it to the gilt cage that would be their new home. Tempting slabs of meat had been placed in their golden prison to lure the tigers from one cage to another.

If Count Orlov had been at Khrenovsky he might have ordered that the tigers live in the palace, despite the terror that the man-eaters inspired. Fortunately the Empress had sent her Lord Admiral of the Black

Seas to destroy the Turkish navy, and until the Count returned, the tigers were confined in their gilt cage on the lawn.

Even after the beasts were behind golden bars the serfs were afraid of them. At mealtimes they refused to get close and instead would throw the bones from a distance at the tigers. Soon there was a scattering of meat bones that had bounced off the bars, littered around the grass surrounding the cage.

Only one person in the palace was brave enough to approach them. Each day, Anna would quietly creep closer and closer to the tiger cage. She calmly faced the snarling beasts, letting them get slowly accustomed to her presence. And then one day she summoned up the courage to pick up one of the wasted bones and gently push it between the bars.

If her pulse quickened at this act, it was purely from excitement at being so close to such glorious creatures. Anna began to feed the tigers daily, and afterwards she would sit cross-legged right outside their cage as if they were the sun and she was basking in their light. She loved the feline grace of their movements, the way they padded about their enclosure, so enormous and yet so silent, their hips swaying gently, long stripy tails trailing out behind them. Her heart was so full of joy at their beauty there was no room left in it for fear.

The tigers seemed to sense Anna's kindred nature. Veronika and Valery, named so by Anna, lay down on the floor of their golden prison, barely twitching their tails while she lay on her belly on the other side of the bars. They were utterly content in each other's company. Unlike the bears, the tigers also seemed to be well matched. Anna could see from the way they rubbed against one another and gave each other playful cuffs with their enormous paws that they had a happy relationship.

It was easy to tell them apart. The male tiger was far larger and his face was broader. The female was smooth and sleek with a distinctly regal beauty. The black stripes of her arched eyebrows reminded Anna of the kohl brows her mother drew on as part of her make-up for dinner parties.

She had never told her mother about what had happened the night she tried on the necklace. She had put the black diamond hastily back in its case, and since then the stone had remained there. The next time it was brought out, her mother would place it round Anna's neck herself. However, that moment would not bring Anna the joy that she expected. Instead, it was the worst moment of her life.

Winter had set in at the Khrenovsky estate. Snow covered the topiary on the palace lawn and the gilt cages were draped in heavy tarpaulins to provide some shelter for the animals within. The bears and the foxes were in hibernation. The tigers, who lived snowbound for most of the year in the wild, took it in their stride. Inside the palace, the exotic creatures were kept warm by the roaring stoves, the fires stoked constantly.

"We must bundle you up," the Countess would tell Anna as she wrapped her in woollens and furs before she was allowed outside, "otherwise you shall fall ill."

However, it was not Anna but the Countess who succumbed to sickness. In the week before Anna's tenth birthday her mother developed a raging fever that drove her to bed. By the third day, when the

Countess was still bedridden, Anna began to worry.

"We should send for the doctors," she told Ivan. "Mama is getting worse. It might be pneumonia."

"So you have diagnosed her yourself?" her older brother sneered. "Well, we don't need the doctors now, do we?"

"Ivan!" Anna said. "This is serious."

Ivan rolled his eyes. "The snowfall is too heavy – the doctors will never come in this weather. Let the housemaids do some work for once and care for her."

Anna couldn't help but think that her brother secretly delighted in their mother's illness. With their father away at sea fighting the Turks, Ivan considered himself in charge. With the Countess confined to her room and Katia in constant attendance on her, Ivan demanded the kitchen should throw away the dinner they had made and produce his favourite meatballs instead. When the food came he pushed aside his cutlery and ate greedily with his hands, smearing grease on his shirt front.

"Come on, Anna," he taunted her. "Let's have some fun for once. How about a swordfight?"

"No, thanks." Anna tried to leave the table.

"Where do you think you are going?" Ivan's mood shifted suddenly from playful to threatening. "If you won't play, you can at least stay and keep me company."

And so she was forced to sit in her chair while he grabbed his sabre and leapt around on the dining-room table, skidding in his jackboots on the polished wood, kicking plates and glasses aside so that they crashed to the floor, laughing like a madman.

Anna watched her brother anxiously and felt gnawing panic rise in her. While Ivan played master, their mother's health was growing worse by the hour.

"We need to send for doctors," Anna tried insisting again.

"All right!" Ivan groaned. "Only will you stop complaining? You are giving me a sore head."

By the time the physicians arrived the situation was grave.

"Send a messenger to your father, Count Orlov," Anna overheard the head physician telling Ivan. "He must return immediately if he wants to see his wife alive."

As the Countess's condition deteriorated Katia was a constant presence at her mistress's side, mopping the Countess's brow and holding her hand to ease the pain.

It was Katia who came to Anna, her face ashen, and told her that her mother was asking for her. Anna found herself walking as if in a dream, towards her mother's chambers. The Countess looked so thin and frail from her illness, but still beautiful.

"Is that you, *milochka*?" Anna's mother raised her head from the pillow and put out her hand to clasp her daughter's fingers.

"It's me, Mama," Anna said, her voice trembling.

The Countess smiled. "Dearest one. Come here and take my hand."

Anna was surprised by the coldness of her mother's fingers, like icicles against her skin.

"*Milochka*," her mother instructed. "I need you to do something for me."

"Anything, Mama."

"My black diamond necklace. You will find it in the top drawer of my dresser. Bring it to me?"

Anna did as her mother instructed, carrying over

the necklace in its velvet case and placing it on the bedside.

"Open the box," the Countess instructed.

Anna carefully prised it open and the Countess reached in and took out the priceless jewel. "The Orlov Diamond," she said, "has been in our family for many centuries. My mother gave it to me and her mother before her…" She turned to Anna.

"And now *milochka*, it will be yours."

Anna's eyes filled with tears. "No, Mama, I do not want it any more."

"Anna." Her mother's voice was gentle. "Please, let me see how it looks on you."

Not knowing what else to do, Anna bowed her head in obedience as the Countess weakly raised herself up off the pillows to clasp the necklace round her daughter's pale neck.

"So beautiful!" the Countess breathed. And then she added, "But it is not the first time you have worn it, is it? That night in my room. You tried it on."

Anna nodded. "I did."

"So you already know that this is no ordinary

necklace." The Countess nodded wisely. "Well, know this too, dear one. You must never seek to understand its power, and do not try to control it. Past and present and future all lie within this necklace, but it is the stone that decides what you will see."

The Countess looked very sad, and then gripped her daughter's hand even more tightly. "Anna," the Countess said. "Your father…"

"He is coming, Mama," Anna tried to reassure her. "We have sent for him, he is on his way!"

The Countess shook her head. "No, my dear one, I know he is not. He will not come for me." The Countess's expression was dark. "I know your brother too. He is so different from you, Anna. I wonder how it is that I could have raised two children, one so lovely and one so…" the Countess drew a sharp breath and began to cough. Anna had to help her sit up, adjusting the pillows so that she could breathe again.

"Look to Katia," the Countess whispered the words. "Katia will care for you. If you are ever in any doubt about what to do, go to her. You can trust her with your life…"

"Mama…" The tears rolled down Anna's cheeks. "Please do not talk like this. You are going to be fine, you will get well again…"

It was Katia who found them.

Anna was slumped and sobbing, still clutching her mother's cool hand. Katia raised the white sheet of death over the Countess's face and hugged and comforted Anna. Ivan was nowhere to be found.

"I went hunting," he told Anna when she asked where he had been. "It would have made no difference if I had been here, would it? It was always you that she loved."

Anna was shocked. "Do you really think Mama didn't love you?"

Ivan laughed harshly. "What do I care? Anyway it was a good hunt. I bagged a deer. So don't try and make me feel guilty about it."

"You do not care that she died without you or father beside her?" Anna said.

"Our father is Admiral Lord Commander of the Black Sea," Ivan sniffed. "He does not run to his wife's bedside like a weakling when there is a war to be won."

With no mother and no sign of their father's return, Ivan took it upon himself to rule the Khrenovsky estate. He started wearing the Count's greatcoat inside the house, even though he must have been baking hot. The huge garment swamped his lean thirteen-year-old frame. He would stalk the corridors, laughing to himself and barking ridiculous orders at the serfs. And the servants began to call him "Ivan the Terrible" behind his back. As for Anna, she avoided her brother as best she could, spending most of her time down at the stables with the horses and Vasily. It was there that she heard the news that her father was finally coming home.

The war, in fact, had been over for some time. Count Orlov could have sailed home several months ago, but instead had delayed his return by deciding to travel overland. The reason for his change of plans was a horse.

"His name is Smetanka," Vasily told Anna. "It has taken his men almost a year to walk him through the mountains from Turkey into Russia. The Count joined them on the coast of the Black Sea and he is personally escorting the horse on the final leg of the journey home."

"My father didn't come home to my mother because he was walking a horse?"

Vasily tried to soften the blow. "Smetanka is not ordinary horse. He is purebred Arabian stallion. They say he cost Count Orlov 60,000 roubles!"

The price of Count Orlov's Arabian was the talk of the palace. At the stables the grooms spoke of nothing else. "What kind of horse could be worth such money?" Yuri, the head groom, could not disguise his scorn. "I could buy a hundred of the best stallions in Russia for that!"

"If he is truly great stallion he will be worth it," Vasily replied.

"Did I ask your opinion?" Yuri had snapped back.

Yuri resented the junior groom's gift with horses and yet he could not get rid of him. Vasily was the most talented horseman in the Count's stables. So Yuri made him work twice as hard as the rest. It was Vasily alone whom the head groom charged with the task of preparing the stable for the Arabian's arrival. And Vasily who was sent out to meet Count Orlov's party at the gates of the estate.

Anna went with him, desperate to see this "very special" horse that had kept her father away during their darkest days. For hours she stood at Vasily's side as the snow fell, and then finally when the night was drawing in, she saw riders in the distance. There were about a dozen men on horseback. Count Orlov rode at the head of the party and when Anna saw the horse that her father sat astride she was bitterly disappointed.

Smetanka looked so plain! A chestnut with a narrow chest, Roman nose and stocky limbs "He does not look like he is worth a hundred roubles even!" Anna muttered.

"Oh no, Lady Anna." Vasily shook his head. "That horse, he is not Smetanka! Look! The grey stallion, in the middle with no rider, *that* is him…"

The Count was not foolish enough to ride his valuable new acquisition on treacherous roads. Instead, he had reined Smetanka in the midst of his riders, surrounded by a cluster of mounted soldiers. The ruse was pointless, however, because alongside the soldiers' ordinary, thickset carthorses, Smetanka's singular, exquisite beauty stood out like a shining star, so bright it eclipsed them all.

He was the colour of highly polished silver and his coat looked as if it had been buffed to the sheen of precious metal. His neck arched like a fountain, and his limbs were so fine and delicate it seemed impossible that those slender legs had journeyed over the mountainous terrain of Turkey. And yet even though he had been travelling for the better part of a year, Smetanka strutted out with the flamboyance of a dancer, as if he were sashaying to some unheard music, sinew and muscle rippling under his glistening coat.

Just as she had been instantly intoxicated by the sight of the Siberian tigers, Anna now found herself falling in love all over again. It was not just the physical beauty of the stallion that drew her, but something deeper. His dark eyes spoke to her deeply and she was reminded of the way she had felt gazing into the black teardrop diamond for the first time.

Instinctively she felt for the necklace at her throat, grasping the stone tight in her fingers. It was a reflex, a habit she had developed to soothe herself ever since her mother passed away. Had it really been a whole month since her death? Anna had been so desperately lonely without her. She had not seen her father in almost a year.

The horses shook their manes, bits clanking in their mouths. They were snorting and blowing from their long journey. Count Orlov, his cape dusted with snow, fur hat pulled down low across his brow, dismounted from the narrow-chested chestnut and walked towards his daughter. For a long while, he said nothing at all, and Anna did not dare to speak. Any words she might have wanted to say were knotted tight in her throat.

"You have grown," Count Orlov said, without any emotion in his voice. "And yet, with my blood I would have expected you to be taller still."

A look of annoyance crossed his face. "Why are you here, child? And where is my son?"

It took Anna a moment to find a reply.

"My brother, Father?"

The Count gritted his teeth. "Yes, your brother. Where is he?"

"Ivan is at the palace, Father."

Count Orlov cast a glance at Vasily. "Take the Arab to the stables. See that he is well looked-after. It is colder here than he is accustomed to." And then, without another word to Anna, the Count remounted his horse. He set off at a gallop, his men closing ranks behind him, heading for Khrenovsky Palace, his home and his son, the only child who mattered.

CHAPTER 4

Boris and Igor

Hot-blooded Smetanka had not been bred to survive the bitter cold of a Russian winter. As the weather became bleak and the coarse carthorses grew thick, shaggy fur, the Arabian remained fine-coated, shivering and miserable. When the snowdrifts gathered outside his stall, Vasily piled the horse with layers of rugs to try to keep him warm. All the same, the cold chilled Smetanka's bones, and the stallion rapidly lost condition. By February he was reduced to nothing but rib and sinew.

"I worry for him," Vasily confided to Anna. "He is so thin and always anxious. When I arrive at the stables before dawn he is always at the door of his stall. I have not once seen him sleep."

For a few hours each day, Vasily would take the stallion out of his stall and let him loose in the small field near the stables. This was the time that Anna most looked forward to. She loved to see the Arabian in motion, the flamboyance of his high-stepping trot and the smoothness of his canter. Smetanka, unaccustomed to the snow, found the cold drifts around his legs intolerable. He elevated himself with every stride, as if he could not bear to make contact with the ground for more than a split second. To gallop with his tail held erect and his head high was the only respite for poor, unhappy Smetanka.

"He hates it here," Anna told Vasily. "I can sense the homesickness in him."

Vasily did not argue. "Lady Anna, his blood is high born, bred for the desert." He shrugged. "Heat and dust are all he has known his whole life. To be brought here to the bleakness and the cold, it is no wonder he is so unhappy."

Yuri would not listen when Vasily tried to tell him how depressed Smetanka had become.

"Oh very sad, it is," he mocked. "Poor horse, waited on hand and foot. I should be so lucky to be priceless Arabian instead of worthless head groom!"

Yuri's dislike of Smetanka only deepened when Count Orlov tasked his head groom with finding a potential mate for the prized stallion. Yuri began by parading a selection from the Count's own stables for consideration. He was dismayed when Count Orlov rejected every single one of them.

"Inferior!" The Count waved them all away with a dismissive hand. "None of them are worthy of my stallion! Increase your efforts and widen your search!"

Next, Yuri sent his riders out to hunt for mares, first to farms around Moscow, and then the whole of Russia, but without success.

"You bring me another ugly cart-beast!" Count Orlov fumed. "I am trying to breed the best carriage horse in Russia and you, Yuri, bring me pig-slops as his bride!"

In the end, it was Count Orlov himself who found Smetanka's perfect match. The mare's name was

Galina, and she was a carriage horse from St Petersburg. Dark brown with a very pretty face and four white socks, Galina was descended from the Empress's carriage stallion.

"She has strong legs and a powerful chest," Count Orlov assessed. "Let us hope she will pass on these traits when her blood mingles with Smetanka's."

The merging of bloodlines was an obsession for the Count. Anna was beginning to notice how often her father spoke of breeding, not just in his animals but in humans too. If he singled out a noble of the royal court to comment upon he would always note their "blood" and whether it was good or not. To the Count, the blood you carried inside you was of the utmost importance, as were your physical attributes. Anna, with her blonde hair, lithe limbs and pale ivory skin, could not help but resemble the Countess.

"Your mother was of excellent blood, descended from royalty," Count Orlov had told Anna as they watched Yuri parading yet more unsuitable mares. Anna was surprised to hear him speak of her mother at all. From the moment of his return to Khrenovsky,

Count Orlov had insisted that every trace of the Countess be removed from the palace. It was as if she had never existed. Her portraits were taken down from the walls and her room was cleared out. Anna had been devastated to discover that all of the Countess's beautiful evening gowns had been disposed of, burned on a pyre. She would have so loved to keep them, so that one day she could wear them to grand balls in opulent palaces just as her mama had done. But Count Orlov made sure that nothing was left. The black diamond jewel which Anna wore at her neck was the only memento of her beloved mother.

***

As the icicles froze solid on the bare limbs of the trees it became clear that Galina was in foal. The tigers too, were expecting a cub. Anna was the one who saw the signs of pregnancy before anyone else. She noted how Veronika, the tigress, was so grumpy, snarling and growling at Valery for no good reason. Then the swell of the tiger's waist confirmed it. There was a cub on the way.

Anna spent every minute she could with Veronika. She would set up camp on the lawn and Katia would ferry out her breakfast and lunch on a tray, only insisting that her young charge came back in at nightfall for dinner. Even Clarise gave in to Anna's pleas and agreed to tutor her as she sat beside the cage – albeit shouting her instructions from the safety of the terrace – so that Anna could watch and wait for the baby tiger to be born.

One day Vasily came up to visit her and found Veronika pacing the bars while Anna pressed right up to them, stroking the plush fur of the gigantic cat as she swept by.

"Do you want to lose an arm?" he asked, horrified. "Pull your hand out! She is about to attack!"

The tigress was emitting a strange, deep growl. It sounded fearsome, but Anna knew better. "Listen! Do you hear that?" She smiled. "Veronika is purring to me!"

All the same, Vasily dragged her away from Veronika, enlisting Anna's help down at the stables.

"Your father has ordered me to break in Smetanka so that the stallion can be ridden under saddle,"

Vasily explained. "I need a lightweight rider to put on his back the first time."

"Me?"

"You are a good size, Lady Anna."

"But I have never broken a horse before," Anna said.

"I have seen you ride every horse in this stable," Vasily replied. "You have a good seat and kind hands. You are never afraid and I have never seen you fall. I think you will do."

As they approached the stables, Anna's stomach was tied in knots.

Smetanka fretted and stamped in the loose box as Vasily put on his saddle and bridle. Anna watched the stallion moving about restlessly and marvelled at his beauty. Smetanka could have been carved from marble. Anna stepped up to the horse, admiring the way his ears pricked in a curve so that the tips came in and almost touched. She delighted in the way his nostrils widened with excitement, taking snorty, anxious breaths. Instinctively she crouched down in front of him and put her face close to his muzzle, and then she breathed too, long and low, deep and slow breaths. Soon Smetanka's breathing slowed down too until they were both calm.

Anna reached out her fingers to stroke the stallion's beautiful dished nose. "Don't be anxious," she told him. "We are going to have fun together, you and I."

Vasily led the horse out of the stables into the field beyond. The snow was falling lightly, and Smetanka shook his mane repeatedly.

"Do not ask too much of him today," Vasily said to Anna. "Walk him perhaps, or trot a little, no more than that. It is his first time with a rider on his back."

Anna raised her leg, signalling that she was ready, and Vasily took hold of her thigh and boosted her up.

Smetanka surged forward at the strange sensation of weight on his back, and he danced a little, but he did not buck or rear or try to run. When Anna took up the reins and began to steer him, guiding him with her hands and her legs, he soon understood what he was required to do. It was not long before she was walking him without Vasily at her side, and then trotting him. His paces floated above the ground as if he were lighter than the air itself!

"It is like riding a cloud!" she giggled.

Vasily frowned. "Be careful," he warned her. "He is very powerful. That is enough for one day, I think. Slow him and bring him back to me."

But Anna was having such fun on the horse that she was no longer listening. Smetanka was so biddable, so clever, and she felt so safe on him. She gave a quick pulse of her legs and cried out with delight as Smetanka responded by breaking into a canter. The fluid beauty of his stride suspended her and she could think of nothing else except the wonderful feeling of flying. For the first time since her mother's death, she was happy.

Anna never wanted to come down again, but she knew that she could not ride Smetanka forever. Besides, Vasily was now shouting at her to halt. So eventually, she turned the magnificent stallion back to the stables and cantered him all the way until they were at the gates.

"He is amazing," she told Vasily as she dismounted and passed him the reins.

"He is a great horse," Vasily said. "And a very valuable one. You must listen to me next time, Lady Anna. Do not go racing off like that! 60,000 roubles and you treat him as if he is your riding pony!"

Never mind that Vasily was grouchy with her, Anna was elated by her ride. She made the long walk back to the palace, feeling the pleasant ache of her tired muscles. Katia had drawn a bath and laid out a dinner gown on her bed. After she had changed and brushed her hair, Anna went downstairs to the main dining room.

Since his return to the Khrenovsky estate, Count Orlov had seldom made time to have dinner with his children. In the grand dining room, at a table large enough to seat thirty guests, Anna and Ivan ate alone. Anna had given up trying to engage her brother in conversation at these dinners – usually he sat at the far end of the table and refused to speak to her. Today, however, when she entered the dining room, Ivan called out to her.

"Anna! Come over here!"

It was a little strange that he called out but did not stand up from his chair in the usual gentlemanly fashion to greet her. Then she noticed the golden bundle of fur on his lap.

"What is that you have?" she asked anxiously, her breath caught in her throat.

"It is my new toy." Ivan looked smug.

Anna stepped closer, hardly believing her eyes. The bundle on Ivan's lap was moving! She saw a little face rise up, black stripes against burnt amber fur, a pink button nose and tiny eyes jammed closed in newborn blindness.

"Ivan! How did you get him?"

Anna moved closer, arms outstretched, but Ivan raised a hand to shove her away.

"He's mine and you can't touch him. Father said so."

"You have Veronika's cub!" Anna gasped. "Ivan – he is a new-born living creature, not a toy! He should still be with his mother!"

"His mother?" Ivan hissed. "Hah! His loving mother is the one who tried to kill him!"

"You are lying!" Anna was shocked. "Veronika would never do that!"

"Yes, she did!" Ivan shot back. "I saw her. He

had only just been born and I saw her grasp him with her teeth and try to eat him!"

Anna groaned in disbelief. "Ivan, don't you know anything about tigers? She wasn't trying to eat him! She was carrying him. Tigers pick their cubs up by the scruff like pussycats do."

"No, she wasn't!" Ivan's face had turned crimson with rage. "She was biting him!" he said. "If it hadn't been for me getting rid of her this cub would be dead."

Anna's blood ran cold. Had Ivan hurt Veronika?

"Don't worry," Ivan scoffed. "The vicious tigress is still alive. I sent the cowardly serfs into the cage and they lured her off with fresh meat while I grabbed the cub."

"Ivan!" Anna pleaded. "You must give him back! Veronika will be heartbroken!"

"*Niet!*" Ivan shook his head. "He is mine now. Father has given him to me."

"What?" Anna couldn't believe it. "You've never shown the slightest interest in the tigers before now! What will you do with a tiger?"

Ivan picked the cub up with one hand so that he

could drape his napkin over his lap in preparation for the meal. Then he raised the cub in front of his face. The baby was still blind to the world, his new-born eyes shut tight. "I am going to train him to eat you. Aren't I, kitty?"

"Is that supposed to be funny, Ivan? Because—"

The door to the dining room swung open and Katia came in bearing a large silver platter filled with meats and caviar.

She put the platter down, and then as she left the room Ivan plonked the tiger cub on the dining table. He left the tiny creature tottering about blindly on wobbly paws while he picked up his fork and began to stab at the slices of meat, transferring them to his plate.

"Ivan, *niet*!" Anna was horrified.

"What?" Ivan glared at her. "Don't make a fuss. He can stay on the table while we eat, he's quite clean."

"I am not worried about that," Anna replied. "He is too close to the table edge – he might fall."

Ivan laughed. He reached out with his fork and gave the tiger cub a sharp poke in the ribs. "Get back, kitty!"

The tiger cub mewled in distress, and Ivan laughed and jabbed him again. He had that familiar cruel smile on his face; Anna knew the expression only too well.

"Please, Ivan. Stop it!"

"He likes it!" Ivan gave the cub another jab with the fork.

"You're hurting him," Anna cried.

"Shall we build him an obstacle course?" Ivan began to set up objects on the table in a circle round the cub – salt-shakers and cream jugs, a large bowl of black caviar. Then he began to poke the cub over and over with his fork, making him take a step forward, then sideways, then another forward again.

With each jab the cub would mewl pitifully. He staggered about while Ivan continued to delight in his torture. "You see? I am training him!"

Anna couldn't take it any more. She stood up from her chair, raced to Ivan's end of the dining table, and carefully took hold of the cub's tiny body.

"Give him to me… owww!"

Ivan had jabbed his fork into the back of Anna's hand.

"Argh! Are you insane?" Anna jerked her hand to her chest. She could see three drops of blood welling up where he had broken the skin.

"My tiger!" Ivan's face turned dark. "Go get your own toys if you want to play."

Anna was trembling, biting back tears. Wouldn't Ivan love it if she cried? The poor cub was mewling once more in terror. She wanted so badly to pick him up but Ivan still had his fork poised like a weapon in his balled-up fist.

"I wish you were not my brother," she said.

Ivan laughed. "You know your problem, little sister? You are too sensitive!"

He used his napkin to wipe the tines of his fork and then he speared another piece of meat and continued to eat.

***

If the Countess had been there she would have told Ivan off for his cruelty and taken the tiger cub from him. But Anna's mama was gone, and Count Orlov had already given the tiger to Ivan. So what could she do? Anna could never go against her father's wishes. And besides, her older brother was the rightful heir to the estate at Khrenovsky. In Count Orlov's eyes, Ivan could do no wrong.

Watching her cruel brother torment the tiger cub every day was unbearable but Anna knew that if she tried to rescue the poor creature it would make things worse. Her only hope was Ivan's fickle nature. She would pretend she didn't care for the cub at all, and ignore his teasing. In time, as with everything else, Ivan would tire of his "plaything".

Ivan tested her resolve. He became increasingly cruel in his attempts to provoke her. He would look Anna in the eye as he pulled the tiger cub's tail, then yank the creature's whiskers so hard they came clean out in his fist. His favourite trick was to pick the mewling cub up by his ears and swing him at Anna so that she had to run from the room.

One morning, when Anna thought she could no longer handle sitting through another meal with him, Ivan arrived at the table without the cub.

Anna knew better than to react. *Do not mention the tiger. Do not arouse suspicion.*

She struck up a conversation, determined not to let her brother know her mind was racing. "I was down at the stables with Vasily," Anna said. "He told me that Yuri was preparing horses for father to go hunting today."

"I know that!" Ivan snapped. "I am going hunting with him!"

And so it was that Anna found herself alone in the palace, finally able to go on a hunt of her own.

She found the stripy cub bewilderedly wandering the hallways and bent down straight away to pick him up. The young tiger flinched back and let out a pitiful mewl.

"Don't be scared," Anna cooed softly. "I would never hurt you!" And then she ran to find Katia in the scullery.

"Please, Katia, I need to find something to feed the tiger cub. He is hungry," Anna asked when she found the head housemaid in the scullery.

Katia headed to the kitchen and retrieved a bowl filled with goat's milk.

"Come on, Boris," Anna tried to coax him. "Come and eat."

The tiger, not yet knowing the name Anna had bestowed on him, but certainly smelling the milk, crawled forward on his belly, emitting a tiny version of the same purr that his mother used to make whenever Anna sat close to the bars of her cage.

He gave the milk a sniff and then lapped it up hungrily while Anna stroked him and murmured. "That's it, Boris, good boy…"

The tiger cub was Boris from that point on; *Borenka* when he was being especially sweet and playful. The cub was so gentle-mannered, he would retract his claws so that he did not scratch her when they had play fights. Made bold by Anna's kindness, he grew more playful and confident every day. Yet the very sight of Ivan striding down the corridor was enough to make the young tiger run and cower.

"I know how you feel," Anna told the cub. "He is my brother and I am the same way."

Boris grew fast. He was almost as tall as Anna's knee when Igor the wolfhound puppy swelled their ranks to a threesome.

The borzoi was the result of Count Orlov's efforts to breed a hunting hound that could take down a timber wolf and outrun a jackrabbit. His bloodline mastery had produced a sleek, lean animal – a champion wolfhound.

Count Orlov's skill as a breeder was the talk of the royal court. How was it that he could produce such miraculous breed specimens? What was the secret to his ability to shape their bodies and their minds?

Anna was aware of the whispers about *Le Balafre* amongst the serfs too. They spoke about his methods in dark tones, hushing as soon as Anna was within earshot.

"Why do they always go quiet when I am in the room?" she asked Katia.

The head housemaid paused and then she said softly, "Your father is a powerful man, Anna. He is like a god in the way he can create life and bring death. His animals are the most beautiful in Russia – but their perfection has a price. And you would do best to not ask too many questions."

Later, Anna would think how ironic it was that her father's powers to mould his creatures' minds had failed completely when it came to Igor's nature.

Count Orlov had bred the borzoi to be a ruthless hunting machine, a bloodthirsty killer, and yet Igor was a resolutely gentle creature and Anna's most loyal companion.

Anna had been at the kennels the day Igor was born. He was the only snow-white pup in a litter of eight grey-and-white siblings. The runt of the litter, weak and forlorn, Anna had fallen in love with him straight away and had begged the houndmaster to give him to her. The houndmaster, thinking that Count Orlov would not miss such a scrawny weak pup, had agreed, and Anna had carried the snowy ball of fur back home to the palace.

Igor soon grew to be taller than any of his brothers and sisters, and faster than any other hound. Despite his strength and speed, he remained as docile as a kitten. It would never have occurred to Igor that he might try to hunt any of the animals he encountered careening around the corridors of the palace. He romped happily with the family of minks who had set up residence in the upstairs bedrooms. He played an endless game of peek-a-boo with the cheeky otter siblings who lived in the stream that ran through the estate. And he kept a respectful distance from the pair of Amur leopards who continued their reign, wandering the halls wherever they liked, still dressed as if for an elegant *soirée* in their black velvet collars.

Anna had worried that there might be a rivalry between the pup and Boris, but from the moment they met the borzoi and the tiger cub became firm friends. Anna would often walk through the gardens with the pair of them at her heels. She had fashioned a white silk velvet collar for Igor, but for Boris, she would remove her diamond necklace, placing it round the tiger cub's ruff. She loved the way his deep orange fur refracted through the black gem, its brilliant facets reflecting an otherworldly amber glow, as dark and mysterious as the eyes of the tiger who wore it.

As Boris grew, his unchecked presence in the palace became terrifying for the servants. They could not believe that Anna could truly control the gigantic beast. And yet Anna never feared her tiger. She knew that he was loyal, that he would do anything to protect her.

She could not have foreseen that Boris's devotion was dangerous for both of them. In the end, it would tear them apart.

CHAPTER 5

Dark Water

Anna woke that morning to a blood-red sky. Outside, the Khrenovsky estate was covered in a thick blanket of snow and the air was so cold her breath froze as she walked the long driveway that led to the stables.

She strode out with a sense of purpose, partly to warm herself, but also because she needed to get to the stables before Vasily. The groom had been so tense and uptight when she had ridden Smetanka. No wonder the poor stallion was so miserable – he was never allowed to feel his own true speed with a rider on his back. Smetanka wanted to gallop, Anna sensed it. He wanted to be free. Now, she was about to show him freedom.

"Smetanka!" Anna called to the horse with a whisper from the stable door. Smetanka raised his head and nickered in reply, then walked over to her. Anna slipped the latch and went inside. The Arabian stallion widened his nostrils and gave an inquisitive snort at an intruder in his stall.

"We are going to go very fast today, you and me," Anna confided as she led him out into the yard. She saddled him quickly, slipped on his bridle and then drew the stallion alongside the mounting post. As soon as he felt the weight of a rider on his back, Smetanka began to skip about anxiously as if there were hot coals beneath his hooves. When Anna tried to hold him still while she slipped her feet into the stirrups, he only danced the more. Once she had her stirrups, she rode him forward. Anna kept a firm grip on his head, which was held high, champing against the bit. They were heading down through the snow-covered meadows that led to the Voronezh River.

As Smetanka jogged and snorted beneath her, Anna became aware of how quickly he responded as she tapped him with her heels, and how he drew back and arched his neck if she put pressure on his mouth. He was so sensitive, and so delicate, his body so lithe compared to the chunky, broad-bellied carthorses in the stables. No other creature was his equal at the Khrenovsky estate, or in all of Russia, for that matter. And to think that the beautiful Galina was heavy with Smetanka's foal. Would the baby be like his sire? Would he possess the same fire and spirit that made Smetanka so incredible?

The stallion moved with elevated strides through the deep drifts of snow towards the black expanse of the river.

The Voronezh River ran through the very heart of the Khrenovsky estate. Wide and deep, it flowed swiftly in the summer, and threatened to flood its banks as it swelled in the springtime. In the winter, however, the river grew sluggish. Ice floes clogged the waterways and soon these began to join together into one solid mass until the whole of the river had frozen over. That was how the Voronezh was now; a black slick of ice smothered the surface from shore to shore, so thick that Count Orlov used the surface as a winter racetrack. While the rest of the estate was impossible to traverse in the snowy months, the black ice made the perfect surface for carriages, smooth and wide enough for the horses to stride out side by side. A good horse was needed, of course, one that was surefooted enough to stride across the slippery ice. Smetanka was a desert horse and the ice was foreign to him, yet Anna felt certain that his natural grace and athleticism would prove itself on the river.

But first she had to convince Smetanka. When they reached the river's edge the stallion refused to set foot on the ice, sensing the danger of the rock-hard sheet, the darkness of the water beneath.

"It's all right," Anna reassured him. "It is solid. You will see."

She kept her legs wrapped firm round his belly and began clucking and coaxing. Smetanka was like an eel, wiggling this way and that, refusing to step forward. At one point he reared up on his hind legs, but Anna was quick to respond and she gave him a slap on the rump at just the right moment. The stallion finally summoned up his courage and, with a snort and a leap, he was on the ice.

The frozen river was glassy and opaque, a black mirror beneath Smetanka's hooves. Anna let him walk at first, allowing him to grow accustomed to the feel of the ice. Smetanka was snorting in consternation, nostrils flared, head held high. Anna kept stroking his neck as he walked, speaking softly to him, talking French, as she felt certain the sweetness of the syllables would calm him. After all, Smetanka was high-born, and French was the language of the royal court.

"*Très bien*, Smetanka," Anna cooed. "You are very brave. Now, do you feel ready to run?"

As soon as Anna closed her legs on him, Smetanka broke into a trot, and before she could ask again he was already in a canter and then galloping. The surge of power thrilled her like nothing she had ever felt in her life. He was magnificent, with the grace of a ballerina and such speed to his strides! For the first time since Smetanka had arrived at the estate, Anna felt that the horse belonged here. As if he were born into a world of ice instead of the desert sand. They were going at a breakneck pace and yet she felt so safe as she urged him to even greater exertions. She delighted in the numbing sensation of the icy winter wind cutting at her cheeks, making her eyes water.

"Go, Smetanka!" Anna rose up out of the saddle and perched herself forward above the neck of the stallion. The sound of his hooves striking against the black ice echoed across the river – a furious thunder as the horse galloped for all he was worth.

Then suddenly Anna felt the world give way. The ice beneath Smetanka's hooves cracked and opened like a black chasm. Anna was plunging down, falling with the horse into the dark water.

The rush of frigid water closing over the top of her head stole her breath away. Anna panicked, churning the black water to white foam as she struggled, thrashing and flailing as she was dragged under.

Above her, where just a moment ago the sky had been clear and blue, there was a frozen ceiling of solid ice.

Anna's sodden clothes were dragging her deeper and deeper into the icy river. As she looked up she saw her diamond necklace floating away from her body, shimmering in the murky water. It was as if the black diamond were determined to defy their shared fate and make it back to the surface on its own. The diamond rose higher in the water and would have slipped loose from her neck and been lost forever if the chain hadn't tangled in Anna's hair. Long blonde strands snagged in the silver filigree. And so the necklace gave up its selfish bid for freedom and drifted around its mistress's throat as she sank down towards the dark depths of the riverbed.

In the growing gloom, Anna could just make out the surface of the ice and the blur of shapes, silhouettes of men moving on the surface. Forgetting for a moment where she was, she tried to shout out to them, "Help me!"

Too late she realised her mistake as icy riverwater forced its way into her mouth. Anna choked, trying to expel the dark fluid and cling on to her last breaths of air. She looked up at the surface and saw that it was receding further and further – or rather that she was still sinking. Her sodden fur coat had cleaved to her skin and was dragging her even deeper.

In a frenzy, she tugged at the coat sleeves. The

heavy fur clung to her as if it were her own skin. Finally she freed herself and watched it tumble through the inky water beneath her.

The surface had become a faraway blur, like the light of a distant star. Black water pressed in from all sides. Anna could not hold her breath much longer. Still she kept fighting the urge to inhale, knowing that once the water filled her lungs it would be over for her. She had to try to get back up there, kick and stroke her way towards the ice above her, but it was so far away. It was so cold. The world was liquid, dark as a moonless sky. Everything was still and quiet.

Then she felt the sudden churn of the water around her. Something was moving through the river, coming in her direction, sending out ripples like a shockwave. Like a ghostly apparition, a silver horse appeared in front of her, stark against the black water, alabaster legs thrashing, mane flowing like luminous riverweed.

Smetanka swam towards Anna, his legs working like pistons. His magnificent silver tail flared out behind him in the jet water like a smoke plume.

Smetanka had the power to reach the surface and she did not. This was her chance and she took it.

As the grey stallion swept by she lunged at his tail and grasped it with both her hands. Smetanka felt the jerk but he was focused on fighting his way to the surface – it didn't matter to him that he was taking Anna in his wake.

Anna held the tail and puffed up her cheeks, holding in the last breath of air that she possessed. She could only hope that they would make it to the surface before she blacked out from lack of oxygen. Above her, she could see the world coming slowly back into focus. The blue of the sky gave her hope in the blackness, made her hang on despite her exhaustion and the cold. They were almost there…

Smetanka broke the surface like a killer whale. He thrust himself out of the water in a great surge, his eyes wild, taking in great gasps through flared nostrils. Around him, the black water of the river boiled as his front legs churned.

Anna surfaced behind him and gasped in a huge choking breath of air. The silence of her underwater world was shattered by the noise of pickaxes smashing ice floes and her father's voice, shouting at his men, "Quickly! Break up the ice. Create a channel so he can swim to shore! We must get him out of there!"

The hole in the ice had already become twice the size it had been when Anna and her horse had fallen through. Count Orlov's men smashed down their axes to break the surface.

"Keep digging!" Count Orlov demanded. "Faster!"

Smetanka swam the narrow ice channel, making for the riverbank, and Anna somehow continued to cling to his tail. She was about to lose consciousness when she felt strong hands grab her by the shoulders, lifting her out of the water. "Anna, it's all right. I've got you."

Anna could hear her father's voice in the fuzzy distance. He was barking orders to get his stallion to the stables and rug him with blankets stuffed with straw. Quickly. Quickly!

And then she heard him shout, "Vasily! Take my daughter to the palace now!"

"Yes, Count Orlov."

It was Katia who answered the door to find Anna blue-lipped and motionless in Vasily's arms.

"Oh, my dear Lady Anna! Is she still with us?" the head housemaid asked.

Nobody expected her to live, and there were many times when even Anna herself truly believed she was about to die. The cold of the river had sunk deep into her bones, and it was as if nothing would ever warm them again. The chambermaids brought metal bedpans filled with hot coals to toast her sheets, they piled on blankets until she was crushed by the weight of them, but still she shivered and trembled with ice in her veins. She kept slipping in and out of consciousness and the room seemed to ebb away, as if her body were sinking down into the mattress beneath her, the bed swallowing her into its depths like the black water of the river.

"*Mama?*"

"*Yes, milochka, I am here…*"

Was it her mother's voice or Katia's?

Whose hand was it that mopped her brow as the delirium came upon her?

Anna reached instinctively to her throat and felt the hard teardrop of the diamond necklace in her frozen hands. She clutched it and warmth surged through her like fire. She closed her eyes and saw blackness. And then the gloom was pierced by the brilliant beams of spotlights and the sound of music.

And then the gloom was pierced by a brilliant beam of the light and the voices were calling once more... *Valentina, Valentina...*

CHAPTER 6

The Academy

The whip cracked like a gunshot, whistling right above Valentina's head. "Move it!" Sergei shouted at her. "No good! You are too slow!"

The ringmaster flung the lash out again, and this time it struck behind Sasha's heels. "Faster! Faster!"

Rehearsals were always like this. Sergei had a short fuse, and although Valentina tried her best to keep him calm, her best was never good enough.

Sergei snapped the whip again and this time he caught Sasha across the rump. Reacting as if a tiger had leapt on to his back, Sasha kicked out. He flung up both hind legs and then surged forward. As he did this Valentina lost her grip on the vaulting saddle.

She went down head first, plummeting right beside Sasha's flying hooves. Any other rider would have been trampled, but Valentina's reflexes saved her. She tucked her arms and head into a ball before she struck the ground. Doing a lightning-fast tumble roll to get clear of Sasha, she kept her momentum and leapt gracefully to her feet right in front of the ringmaster.

"You could have killed me!" Valentina cried. She could feel her blood pounding at the temples.

"Pah!" Sergei dismissed her anger with an arrogant flick of his head. "You fall. Is not my problem! Now ride the trick again and do not be so slow this time!"

Valentina looked over at Sasha. The pink horse was waiting for her, his sides heaving in and out like bellows. He was lathered in sweat. They had been training like this for over two hours.

"Sergei," Valentina begged, "we have done enough for today. He is exhausted and so am I! And we have to perform tonight."

Sergei was unmoved. "You will keep doing it until you get it right." He jabbed the end of his whip into her chest, prodding her away as if she were

101

one of his tigers. Valentina knew better than to answer back. She turned and walked to her horse.

"Arrogant brat," Sergei spat after her. "We finish when I say, not before! Stop behaving like snivelling baby, Valentina. Now, show me the new trick."

Valentina wiped her face, took a deep breath and clucked to her horse.

At her cue, Sasha picked up his stride and began to canter round the arena perimeter. Valentina watched him and synced her body in time with his strides, like a girl waiting her turn to leap into a swinging skipping rope. When Sasha struck his mark Valentina broke into a run, up on her toes with both arms over her head, and then launched into a double cartwheel. She tucked her torso and simultaneously leapt, grabbing hold of Sasha's saddle with both hands and doing a third cartwheel up into the air. She finished her arc standing upright on the back of the pink horse.

Valentina could feel her arms shaking with exhaustion and Sasha beneath her was lathered with sweat. Surely Sergei would be satisfied with that performance? She turned to the ringmaster and saw his grouper mouth downturned in a customary frown.

"What are you expecting? A gold medal?" Sergei grunted. "Stop wasting time, Valentina. Get back here and do it again!"

***

That evening there was a full house beneath the big top of the Moscow Spectacular. The crowd had cheered for the clowns and the jugglers. They had applauded the tigers, the monkeys riding dogs and the dancing bears. And now, as the music struck up for Valentina, there was the hushed silence that came with an air of expectation. The acrobat and the pink dancing horse – the stars of the circus whose faces featured on the posters, were about to enter the ring.

The music swelled, and the big top was plunged into blackness. Then the spotlights illuminated the ring, their white beams gathering to focus on the platform at the peak of the roof of the circus tent where the trapeze swung... empty.

The spotlight moved around, searching the skies, looking for the performer who should have been swinging a graceful arc across the tent.

"Where is she? Where is Valentina?"

In the wings Sergei was furious. He turned to the nearest of the clowns milling about backstage. "Go get her from her caravan. Tell her she is in big trouble!"

A few moments later the clown was back with Irina at his side.

"What are you doing here?" Sergei asked Irina. "Where is Valentina?"

Irina looked nervous, almost too afraid to speak.

"Valentina is gone," she said.

"Gone?" Sergei scowled. "What are you talking about?"

"Her clothes are missing," Irina said. "She must have packed a bag after rehearsals…"

From the circus ring came the sound of clapping, a loud steady pounding as thousands of hands came together in unison. Some of the audience began stamping their feet on the wooden floor and soon more feet joined in until the whole crowd were stomping and clapping, shaking the seats, insisting that the act begin. The spotlight kept circling. Where was the star performer?

"Irina!" Sergei snapped. "Go get your costume. You go on with Sasha instead of Valentina tonight. I will deal with her nonsense later!"

Irina didn't move.

"Well?" Sergei glared at her. "What are you waiting for?!"

Irina said nothing. It was the clown who spoke up.

"Sergei, she cannot go on."

"Why not?" Sergei demanded. "It is not that difficult. Valentina is not as irreplaceable as she thinks!"

"Maybe not," the clown agreed, "but Irina cannot perform without horse."

Sergei's face fell.

"Valentina has run away and she has taken Sasha with her."

***

105

The tenement blocks looked like the most miserable place on earth, towers of dirty beige apartments with grey curtains, each building the same as the last. Under a streetlamp, Valentina let Sasha graze on the overgrown weeds that sprouted out of the pavements while she watched a group of school kids playing with an old, deflated football.

"Hey!" One of the kids, his hair shaved short, wearing a singlet and no shoes despite the biting cold of the evening, came running up to her. His three friends trailed behind him, probably because he carried the squishy football under his arm. "Are you giving pony rides?"

"No," Valentina shook her head. She had been walking for hours and she didn't even know if she was going in the right direction. She couldn't read the signposts. Valentina took out the piece of paper in her pocket and showed it to the boy.

"This is where I am going," she said. "It is far?"

The boy held the paper high up under the streetlight. "It is in the city. Too far to walk. You should take the metro."

Valentina rolled her eyes. "So, what about my horse? He takes the metro too?"

The boy wiped his nose on his arm. "I will show you the way if you give me a ride on him."

The other kids gathered round as Valentina lifted the boy on to the horse's back. He looked very small up there, dirty feet dangling at Sasha's sides.

"Why are you going to this place?"

"It is a famous riding school," Valentina replied. "I am going to become a dressage rider."

"That sounds boring," the boy said.

Valentina cocked an eyebrow at him. "You think so?"

"Yeah," the boy said. "When I grow up I am going to have an exciting life."

Valentina looked up at him. "So what are you going to do?"

The boy grinned. "I am going to run away and join the circus."

***

107

The wrought-iron gates with the golden sign looked just like they did in the picture that she had treasured for so long. Through the gratings, Valentina could see lights illuminating the stable blocks and the white buildings of the Federation Academy. She gave the gates a shake, but of course they were locked. She thought for a moment of ringing the bell, but what would she say? It was the middle of the night. The whole Academy was shrouded in darkness. Snow had fallen earlier, and now it was drizzling with an icy rain that made Valentina shiver. She looked at Sasha. The horse was shivering too. Both of them would freeze if they stayed out here all night.

Valentina took a step backwards and looked up. The gates were very high, with piercing metal spikes at the top. Dangerous, but not impossible…

Valentina tied Sasha to the gate by his leadrope and, using his mane to pull herself up, she vaulted easily on to his back. From there, she stood on his rump and raised her hands up above her head. A split second later, she leapt into the air. Her hands hooked expertly through the metal curlicues near the top of the gates and she swung from them like a gymnast. Summoning all her upper body strength, she pushed herself into a pike, doubling herself over so that the soles of her feet were now touching the curlicues, and then she sprang upwards like a cat. She brought her hands down on top of the railing, then flipped up into a handstand. Valentina balanced again before executing a second pike so that her toes came to rest precisely in the slender gaps between the spikes.

With a quick flip she righted herself and was standing on top of the gates. How high above the cobbled courtyard she was! There was a spreading cherry tree in the centre. It was quite a distance from the gates to the boughs, but Valentina had made bigger leaps than that without a safety net. Without hesitation she threw herself off the top of the railing.

As the ground raced up to meet her, she focused on the bough, stretching out until her fingertips managed to wrap round the bare, papery limb of the tree. With a sudden jerk she did a full pike to bring her feet up beside her hands, then flung herself out into mid-air, this time reaching for a lower branch. She swung back, dangled for a moment from the bough, and then dropped lightly to her feet on the cobbles below.

Valentina walked over to the courtyard post and pressed the gate-release buzzer. The wrought-iron gates swung open and she calmly walked Sasha into the compound. "Come on," she murmured to the pink horse as he walked beside her with his nostrils wide and head aloft. "Do not be nervous. This is going to be our new home."

***

"Is she dead?"

"I don't know!"

"Poke her!"

"What? No. You do it!"

Valentina opened her eyes. She was curled up on the straw in one of the loose boxes where she and Sasha had bedded for the night. Peering down at her, faces disturbingly close to her own, were a boy and girl, both with thick mops of dark hair and bright green eyes.

"I told you she wasn't!" the boy said.

He smiled at Valentina. "I'm Oscar Mueller," he said. "And this is my sister Molly."

Years later, when the Mueller twins were grown up, they would fondly recall the strange circumstances in which they first met Valentina, for it was Oscar and Molly who convinced their uncle to give her a chance as a groom. George Mueller, the famous head of the Russian Federation Dressage Team, had taken one look at the runaway circus girl and, as he always did, he went on instinct.

"What I liked about the girl was simple," he would later say. "When I asked her what she knew about dressage, she told me she knew nothing. How refreshing to find myself with a rider who admitted that they were ignorant! I took her under my wing and I never looked back!"

Valentina had fallen on her feet. The circus girl and her pink stallion were about to be given the ride of their lives.

CHAPTER 7

Son of Smetanka

To Anna's bleary eyes, the man at her bedside appeared more like an undertaker than a doctor. He was dressed head-to-toe in black and was prodding at her with cold, bony hands. "You must drink this." He sat her up and forced her to swallow some vile black liquid. "It is a tincture," he said as she coughed. "Good for the circulation."

When Count Orlov entered the room the doctor snapped violently to attention, clicking his heels and bowing in a ridiculous fashion.

"How is my daughter?" Count Orlov asked.

"Your Grace, I am prescribing a course of leeches, to be placed upon the pulse points. They may encourage the blood to flow, but whether she will live... I cannot say." The doctor spoke as if Anna was not in the room. "The girl was in the river a long time. There is nothing more to be done but wait and see."

Anna lay there, her blonde hair spread like an angel's halo on her pillow, skin deathly pale, the blood drained from her cheeks. Count Orlov crossed the room and came to her bedside. He leant down, as if to kiss her cheek, but instead of his lips Anna felt the hiss of his whispered words.

"I have just come from the stables," Count Orlov said. "Smetanka is dead. The frozen river was too much for his Arab blood. But not for you, eh, Anna? The Orlov blood in your veins makes you strong." Her father's voice lowered as his face contorted in rage. "That horse was priceless beyond all measure. I curse the day you were born, Anna. I have lost him thanks to you!"

Anna somehow managed to wait until her father left the room before she wept. Katia implored her not to be so upset, and hugged her close, rocking her from side to side. "He does not mean what he said. He is angry now, but he will calm down eventually. You are his daughter and he does love you, despite his temper."

Anna could not stop sobbing. She clung to Katia and her breath came in faltering gulps. "The tears are not for my father," she told Katia. It was for Smetanka that she cried. They were tears of sorrow and of regret, for if she had not taken him on to the ice that day, then surely the noble stallion would still be alive.

***

Anna was too ill to attend the funeral service for Smetanka. Count Orlov spared no expense in giving his prized stallion a grand farewell. Much later, Anna couldn't help but bitterly compare this extravagance with her mother's quiet burial. The memorial service from which her father had been notably absent.

When the Count was told that the winter ground was too frozen to dig a hole large enough for the horse, he forced his serfs to hack at it with pickaxes for hours on end. Smetanka's tombstone was carved from the finest marble, and proclaimed the Count's stallion "the greatest horse in Russia".

All this time Anna lay limp and exhausted in her bed, with Igor the wolfhound and Boris the tiger maintaining a constant vigil. Boris lay catlike at the foot of her bed while Igor remained always on the floor close to her, whimpering softly, ears cocked and head resting on his paws.

Katia came and went with trays of food, trying to convince Anna to eat. She tried to read to her young patient, to engage her in conversation, but it was useless. Orlov blood was not enough – Anna was fading.

"Today I have brought you a visitor," Katia announced one morning as she walked in with the breakfast tray.

"Who is it?" Anna asked.

"Vasily Shishkin," Katia replied. "The young groom from the stables."

"I am too sick to see him," Anna said.

"No, my lady," Katia was firm. "You are not ill, Anna. You are feeling sorry for yourself. That is why I sent for Vasily. He has something to tell you."

"I said no," Anna replied.

"Too late," Katia said. "He is here."

Anna looked up to see Vasily in the doorway. Dressed in kneeboots and drab work clothes, he looked very wrong in her dainty room with its pretty floral bedspread and duck-egg-blue walls.

"Lady Anna." Vasily knelt on the floor beside her but Anna turned her face away, not ready to meet his eyes.

"I am so sorry, Vasily," she murmured.

"For what?" Vasily was confused.

"For taking Smetanka without telling you, for causing all of this." Anna could not stop her foolish tears. "I think about him every day, Vasily. If he had not got so wet and cold in the river then he would still be alive!"

"Is that what you think?" Vasily shook his head. "Anna, I had told you already how feeble Smetanka had grown. He was a desert horse with a body made for heat and sandstorms, not the taiga with its snow and ice."

Vasily clasped her hand tight. "You are not responsible for his death, Anna. It is the cold Russian winter that took him from us. Even if he had not fallen into the river, Smetanka would never have survived until spring. I know it in my heart."

Anna met Vasily's gaze. "Is that true?"

"I believe so," Vasily said. "His blood had fire in it. He was never destined to be a part of our world." Vasily was silent for a moment and then he said, "But his son is different. He is a true Russian horse – he loves the snow and ice."

Anna could not believe what she was hearing. "His son? Smetanka has a son?"

Vasily nodded. "Galina's colt was born three days ago. He is down at the stables. That is why I have come – to take you to meet him."

***

The walk to the stable block felt like the longest that Anna had ever attempted in her life. Her legs were so weak that putting one foot in front of another was exhausting. She kept stubbornly trying to do it alone, but in the end her knees buckled and she had no choice but to allow Vasily to carry her. Lying limp in his broad arms it seemed as if he felt her weight no more than he would that of a feather. As they walked on, he told her all about the foal. "He feeds so voraciously he has already grown in just a few days," Vasily said. "I have never seen a foal so strong, so full of vigour."

"And what does my father say?" Anna asked. "What does he think of him?"

Vasily took a deep breath. "I have not yet told the Count that the foal has been born."

"Whyever not?" Anna asked.

"You will understand when you see him," Vasily replied.

Two of the stalls in the stable blocks were nursing boxes for a mare and foal, and it was into the first of these, with fresh straw and water, that Vasily had placed Galina and her baby.

Anna peered over the stable door, but the foal was hidden behind Galina. She could not see him at all.

"Come inside," Vasily said softly. "I will fetch him for you."

Anna went into the stall and sank to her knees in

the straw while Vasily went behind the mare and coaxed the foal forward.

"He's a dapple grey, like his father," Vasily said as he ushered the foal towards Anna for the very first time.

The grey coat was the only similarity between father and son that Anna could see at that moment. Unlike the elegant stallion, the foal was gangly and awkward, ill-proportioned. He had an absolutely huge head, held up by a skinny, giraffe neck. His legs were stilt-like and his body was elongated – he must have inherited his sire's extra rib. The slopes of his rump and shoulder were so brutal that they made him look desperately malnourished. Any of these features might have been a little odd in a horse's conformation. The total combination was so blindingly unattractive that Anna found herself almost recoiling.

"He is very ugly." Her own words surprised her.

"He is," Vasily agreed.

"And yet," Anna let her gaze linger on the fuzzy little creature, "such proportions will surely serve him well as a carriage horse!"

Vasily pulled a face. "How so?"

"Those legs!" Anna exclaimed. "Vasily, look at him! They are so long, but the bone is solid, the hooves are broad and the knees are like slabs of rock. He will never go lame and even in the deepest snow or the slipperiest ice he will be surefooted."

Vasily was not so easily swayed. "His proportions are wrong," he pointed out.

"Yes," Anna agreed, "but look, Vasily! His enormous head balances out his narrowness and the long back. These traits will give him even more speed and agility on the ice…"

Her eyes were shining as she turned to the groom. "Let's take him out."

"What? Now?" Vasily asked. "But you have only just got out of bed."

Anna could not be swayed. "Please, Vasily? I want to see him run. Let us do it now!"

She reached out a hand in the gloom of the stable box, and the foal stepped towards her, velvet muzzle meeting the tips of her fingers. Anna was impressed when he did not flinch. "He is brave, and inquisitive," she murmured. "A baby horse who greets a human so willingly is very special. Aren't you, little one?"

They took the foal and Galina out into the yard beside the stables. The colt ran the full length of the field, his strides more powerful than anything Anna could have imagined, striking out with such certainty across the ground. Then he pawed the snow with his front hoof and lay down in the white powder to roll and roll. Standing up again, he shook himself and made flakes fly from his mane like a miniature blizzard. Anna laughed for the first time since that tragic day on the river.

"Did you see that trot? He is faster than any fully-grown carriage horse and he is still just a baby!" Anna was clapping and laughing with tears of joy in her eyes. "He is wonderful!" And then, with genuine bewilderment, she said, "Why have you not told my father of his existence?"

Vasily frowned darkly. "When I saw how deformed he looked, I feared what your father would do. Count

Orlov's breeding methods have no room for failure."

"What are you talking about? What methods?" Anna asked.

"You really don't know?" Vasily said.

Anna shook her head vehemently.

Vasily paused and then he said, "Your father is a killer."

Anna's blood ran cold. "You cannot speak like that," she reprimanded Vasily. "It is treason."

But Anna had heard the rumours. She knew that the serfs whispered about *Le Balafre* behind his back. And as much as they tried to hush themselves in her presence, she knew that they said that Count Orlov had killed Peter the Third so Catherine could ascend her husband's throne.

"Even if what they say about my father is true," Anna hissed at Vasily, "what does it have to do with horses?"

"It has everything to do with horses, and all the animals at Khrenovsky," Vasily replied. "Empress Catherine gifted your father this grand estate for showing unquestionable loyalty. This is a man who is prepared to take a life if it will get him a reward. And he does so with his animals. Did you ever wonder why his breeds are perfected so quickly? Any creature he considers to be inferior is disposed of!"

Anna thought about her father working his bloodline mastery, perfecting his breeds and doing away with any animal that was not good enough. It made sense, and yet still she couldn't believe it.

"Vasily!" she said to the groom. "He is my father!"

Vasily met Anna's eyes with a sorrowful look. "If you do not believe me," he said, "then ask about his famous nickname: *Le Balafre*. How is it that he came to get his scar?"

"I know that already!" Anna said. "It was in a fair duel."

Vasily gave a hollow laugh. "You know what prompted this 'duel'? All the poor soldier did was walk by Count Orlov and forget to salute him. Your father was sent into such a spiral of rage he demanded that the matter be settled with sabres. He did not realise that the young officer was the best swordsman in Russia. They had barely drawn their blades when the young man struck a blow that split open Count Orlov's right cheek. Your father had never been marked in a fight before. When the young officer's back was turned he struck him down mercilessly. And when the young man begged for his life, your father laughed and ordered him to salute. As the officer raised his hand he was struck with the fatal blow."

Anna clutched at her own throat. "You are making this up!"

Vasily shook his head. "Your father is the Lord Commander of the Black Sea, and the master of pure breed bloodlines. He seeks perfection no matter what cost. Do you think that he will look kindly upon this ugly colt? You are a dreamer!"

Anna could not believe him. She could not believe that her father would fail to see the promise that lay within the foal.

"I am fetching the Count," she said. "You will see, Vasily. He is not the monster that you think he is."

***

"Anna! You should not be out of bed, child!" Count Orlov was unimpressed to find his daughter wobbling on her exhausted legs at the doorway of his study.

"I came to get you, Father." Anna was panting with the effort of her walk, leaning against the door jamb. "I came to show you the foal, Smetanka's son! He has been born. He is down at the stables."

*

The closer they got to the yard, the more uneasy Anna felt.

Over the years, she had certainly noticed the strange hush that often fell when she entered a room where the serfs had been talking. She had heard the maids whisper behind their hands about *Le Balafre*. And she had noticed how litters of puppies would be in the kennels one day and then gone the next. Anna knew that the Count was obsessed with bloodlines. All the same... No! She could not believe that of her own father. And besides, Count Orlov had the best eye for a horse in all of Russia – surely

125

he would see the potential in Smetanka's son in just the same way as she had done.

At the stables, Vasily greeted the Count and showed him to the stable box. Anna looked for signs of anger in the groom's face, but all she saw was deep concern.

"I hope I am wrong, Lady Anna, I really do," the groom whispered to her as they watched her father open the stable door and enter Galina's stall.

Suddenly the door swung open once more and Count Orlov exited the loose box. His eyes were narrowed in disgust. He growled with barely concealed rage.

"How is it," he fumed, "that a stallion as beautiful as my Smetanka could have such a feeble sapling for an offspring!"

Count Orlov turned to his daughter. "This is the only foal that Smetanka has bred here and look at him! Worthless! Utterly worthless!"

The Count slammed the door of the stall and summoned Vasily to him.

"This bloodline is to be severed immediately, do you understand?"

"Yes, Count Orlov," Vasily bowed. "As you command."

And without a backward glance, Count Orlov strode off towards the palace, leaving Anna in a sobbing mess on the stable floor.

CHAPTER 8

Hidden Nature

Anna found Vasily in the saddlery room. He had a sabre in his hands and he was working it against the whetstone, grinding the slender curve of the blade with his back to her.

"Lady Anna," he said without turning round. "Please go home."

He focused on the sabre, pushing the blade against the stone, then testing the edge on his finger.

"Please, Vasily," Anna wiped the tears from her face, "you can't kill him."

Vasily rose up and walked past her out of the door and down the stable corridor. She ran after him. "He is just a baby! He has only just been born!"

Vasily kept walking. "I have no choice, Lady Anna. It is your father's order. Do you want me to disobey him?"

"Yes, of course!"

Vasily looked at her in disbelief. "Sometimes, Lady Anna, I think you are the most naïve person I have ever met. Do you not understand what it means to defy Count Orlov?"

"My father would forgive you!" Anna insisted. "You are his best groom."

Vasily tensed his shoulders. "Remember what happened to the soldier who gave him his scar? If he finds this foal alive by morning..."

Anna's expression suddenly changed. "Yes, but what if he doesn't find him?"

"What do you mean?" Vasily said.

"The foal. We could hide him! You have a farm cottage, don't you? On the edge of the woods?"

Vasily nodded.

"We will keep him there," Anna said decisively.

Vasily shook his head. "My farm is a pig farm. There are no stables, just sties."

"He will not know the difference!" Anna said.

"Keep him in your pigsty. It will not be forever. Soon Father will go away again to St Petersburg."

"It is too dangerous, Anna. If Count Orlov knew I had deliberately disobeyed him…"

"He won't know!" Anna's face was flushed with excitement. "I swear. It will be our secret."

"It is a ridiculous plan," Vasily said, shaking his head. He looked down at the sabre in his hand, and then gave a deep sigh as he returned it to its sheath. "And I am a fool, because I agree to it."

***

In the months that followed, Anna would often think of the debt she owed Vasily. It was because of his great kindness that she would resist the urge to say "I told you so," when it came to the colt. For the ugly duckling was quickly becoming a swan. Those giraffe-like legs no longer looked disproportionate. And while the colt's head was still too large, his broad brow spoke of intelligence. His powerful jaw tapered to a narrow muzzle that gave him an exotic quality.

"He has grown handsome," Vasily agreed grudgingly. "But you must admit he is still very strange-looking, no? He is more like a dragon than a horse!"

Like a dragon, Vasily said, and Dragon became his name. Spoken in Russian: *Drakon.*

For the first year of his young life, Drakon was kept in the pigsty. Once she was back to her full strength and with her father attending the Empress at the royal court, Anna visited him every day. She loved walking the long winding forest path through the fir trees to Vasily's house. It was a relief to be away from the palace and the watchful glares of her brother.

"I do not like that you travel the woods alone," Vasily would fuss. "It is not safe."

"I have two very good bodyguards!" Anna would reply.

Boris and Igor were her constant companions on these woodland journeys. The vigilant tiger stuck close to her side, padding silently on his velvet paws, while the wolfhound, still full of puppyish energy, could not resist bounding on ahead, then circling back to rejoin them, pink tongue lolling out of his snowy muzzle, mouth wide open with joy.

Sometimes during these mad dashes through the forest undergrowth, Igor would put up a snow rabbit and give chase. He was without doubt fast enough to catch his prey, but he had no desire to kill. Gentle Igor preferred to simply run alongside the rabbit and then let it go free. Anna knew that despite her father's best efforts to breed the killing instinct into the borzoi, Igor had no bloodlust in him. It would never have occurred to him that he might try to bring down any of the animals he encountered. His play fights with Boris the tiger were simply exuberance.

When Anna had first taken the cub and the wolfhound with her to visit Drakon she had worried that the colt would be terrified of her tiger. Horses and big cats are mortal enemies by nature. And by now Boris was a sizeable beast. Yet perhaps because both Boris and Drakon had been raised motherless they had had no one to advise them in such matters. At their first meeting, after seeing Anna approach with Boris, the colt walked straight up to the tiger and lowered his muzzle, taking deep husky snorts through his wide nostrils, breathing in the foreign scent of the big cat. Boris made sniffing noises, raising his furry face so that the wide pink tip of his nose touched Drakon's muzzle. They both started back at the contact and then, tentatively, Drakon reached his neck out again. This time when their noses made contact the horse let out a friendly snort and Boris, feeling the breeze of the horse's breath on his face, began to purr.

Boris and Igor's friendship had been cemented from the beginning by their protectiveness towards their mistress. Now Drakon was about to join their ranks.

***

The colt was almost two years old when an unexpected test of devotion took place.

Over the months, the colt and Anna had developed their own special game, a variation of tag. Anna would whistle for Drakon as she came through the gate, and then climb up the railings of the fence and wait for the colt to trot up to her. Drakon would come near, getting so close that she could almost touch his muzzle before swerving away. Then, with a playful flick of his head, he would put on a sudden burst of speed and gallop to the other side of the field.

Anna would whistle again but Drakon would hold his ground, refusing to come back. Finally, muscles quivering with expectation, he would shake his head defiantly, leap forward into a gallop, and swooping across the ground with eager strides, return to her once more.

This game of back and forth would continue until Drakon's flanks were heaving. He would eventually give in and meekly come to Anna so that she could stroke him and groom him.

This day however, the game changed.

Boris and Igor had already run off to look for Vasily in the pigsties. Anna was unlatching the gate and was about to enter the field when Drakon came charging directly at her. He had his ears flat back against his head and as soon as he was near he began snorting and flinging out his front hooves violently into the air.

"Drakon, *niet!*" Anna scrambled backwards, climbing up the gate to get away from him. When she tried to step to the ground Drakon flung himself viciously at her, rearing up and stamping down with his front legs.

Shaking with fear, Anna clambered off the gate and ran to the pigsties to fetch Vasily.

"I don't know what is wrong with him…" she sobbed to Vasily, fighting to control her tears. "He tried to attack me. He has gone crazy. You must come!"

Vasily followed her and they found Drakon standing at the gate perfectly quiet and docile, nickering to them softly.

"But I don't understand!" Anna said. "He was so different just a moment ago. He would not let me approach. He was pounding the ground with his hooves."

Vasily stepped forward to take the colt by his halter and then suddenly he leapt back.

"Look!" he said to Anna.

Trampled into the dirt at Drakon's feet, was a viper. The greenish-grey body had been crushed and hacked by hooves so that it oozed brackish blood.

"That is your reason," Vasily said. "Drakon knew the snake was there. He drove you back to keep you safe."

Anna had saved Drakon's life and now the colt had repaid her in turn. His loyalty, like that of Boris and Igor, was unquestionable. His talent, burning deep inside him, had yet to be discovered.

***

In the autumn, Drakon turned three and Anna decided he was ready to be ridden. The ice floes had yet to harden into the winter crust on the river, not that this mattered to Anna. She never wanted to risk a horse's life on the black ice again. They would ride along the riverbank as far as the woods and then loop back. She had saddled Drakon and now she led him through the fields, as Vasily walked alongside her with Boris and Igor.

The tiger had grown to his adult size and he walked with a newfound air of authority. Igor, while also fully grown, was still a pup at heart, and he constantly leapt at Boris, trying to get his friend to play fight with him as they had done in the old days.

As they walked towards the river Boris patiently endured Igor's leaps on his back, and taunting nips at his jowls. That was until finally he lost his temper and delivered a swat with the open flat of his mighty paw that sent the borzoi sprawling.

"*Niet*, Boris!" Anna told him off. The tiger gave her a sullen growl and his shoulders slumped, like a child who had been told off unfairly when their sibling was at fault.

"You should have left them both at home, Lady Anna," Vasily complained. "They will get underfoot."

Anna laughed. "You are so grumpy today!"

Vasily frowned. "I should be at the stables. I have work to do."

"I will bring Drakon back to the stables and help you with the work after this," Anna insisted.

With Count Orlov still absent in St Petersburg and Yuri the head groom with him to care for the Count's personal steed, Anna and Vasily had decided to risk moving the colt to live at the stables. They had slipped him into a spare stall one night, and when morning came none of the other grooms seemed to care where this new addition had sprung from – so long as they were not the ones who had to clean out his loose box. Drakon seemed quite happy in his new surroundings. Having grown up alone in a pigsty, he relished having other horses for company and would spend all day with his head craned over the stable door, nickering and calling out companionably.

"You must stay." Anna smiled winningly. "If Drakon bolts and I cannot stop him you may have to come and fetch us back from Siberia."

She was making jokes, but her hands were trembling. All week she had been preparing Drakon for his first time ridden under saddle. She had broken him in herself, starting by simply leaning across the stallion's back to get him accustomed to the feeling of a rider's weight. Slowly as the week progressed she had tested him further, putting more weight on him and then throwing one leg all the way across his back; then finally straddling him so that she was sitting upright. Once he accepted her, Anna began to work with the saddle. The first time she girthed it on to Drakon, he had startled and given a buck, but soon he realised the device would not hurt him. By the end of the week, Anna had been able to saddle and sit on him and chat away to Vasily as if it were perfectly natural to be on Drakon's back.

Vasily had led her within the enclosed yard by the stables, but out by the river they were in the open countryside. There was no telling how the colt would react.

"Take him as far as the woods," Vasily said, "but keep him to a trot, all right?"

Anna pulled a face. "I thought we wanted to see how fast he could go?"

"Next time maybe," Vasily said. "This is all new to him. If he gets overexcited and bolts, you will not be able to hold him."

"All right, we will trot," Anna promised.

Down by the river, where the wildflowers had been blooming just a few months ago, the threat of the coming snow had turned the ground stark and bare. Soon the fields would be buried beneath white drifts, but today they were perfect for riding.

"Good boy, Drakon," Anna murmured as Vasily

untied his rope. Now her hands on the reins were the only thing holding the stallion back.

"Take him slowly, remember…" Vasily began to advise, but his words were brought to an abrupt stop by a shriek from Anna.

"Sorry!" she called back over her shoulder as Drakon surged forward. "This is his idea!"

The big grey stallion might have been broken in to saddle but no one had explained to him who was in charge. He flung his weight against Anna's hands as he bowled into a trot. She had to resist the urge to grab at the reins and pull him back. If they got into a tug-of-war then Drakon would easily win. Besides, she wanted him to run, didn't she?

She could feel the power in the horse beneath her as his strides began to flow, getting faster and more dynamic as he swept across the riverbank. Anna gave a check on the reins but felt no response. Her promise to Vasily had been meaningless. Any minute now the horse would break out of a trot into a canter and then into a gallop. All she could do was hold on.

Drakon's legs were pumping frantically like

pistons, striking out a furious *tchok-tchok* against the earth. Boris and Igor bounded on alongside him excitedly. Anna kept waiting for Drakon to canter, but miraculously, her stallion did not seem to want to. He kept gaining speed until he appeared to be floating above the ground, his ridiculously long legs flung out in front of him, but he did not break from a trot.

At the curve of the river, Anna rose up in her stirrups and leant down low over his neck, her heart pounding as she urged him to even greater speed. She was no longer trying to rise and sit with the trot: Drakon's strides had become so massive and bouncy that no rider could possibly keep up with their rhythm. And still Drakon kept the pace, striding onwards relentlessly towards the forest.

He was still full of running when they reached the trees, and she sensed at that moment that he could have gone on like this forever. A part of Anna wanted that too, to keep going into the woods, just her, Drakon, Boris and Igor. They would disappear together into the trees and never return to Khrenovsky.

If it had not been for the winter chill in the shadows of the firs that made her shiver, then perhaps Anna would have considered it. The icy air brought her back to reality and she pulled hard on the reins. At last Drakon listened to her, slowing his stride. From a trot to a walk, he came back to her and Anna gave him a firm pat on his sleek, dapple-grey neck. Then, telling him he was a good boy, she turned him round and let the reins hang loose to cool him down on the homeward journey. The stallion gave triumphant snorts, his nostrils flared wide, breath coming like a dragon's with a hiss and rumble of air.

"Wasn't he amazing?" she called out to Vasily as the groom ran along the riverbank to meet them.

Vasily shook his head in disbelief. "He trots faster than most horses can gallop! I have never seen such speed."

"I know!" Anna laughed. "I told you we would trot, didn't I?"

As she loosed Drakon in his stall that night and gave him his feed, Anna was practically dancing with delight. The other horses in the stables put their heads over the doors and nickered their greetings to Drakon.

"Do you hear them calling you?" Anna whispered to her horse. "Shall we tell your friends in the other stalls about how you ran today? Tell them how fast you are?"

Drakon gave his mane a shake as if he were embarrassed by her praise. Anna flung her arms round his neck, holding him tight.

"Wait until my father sees you run like that," she murmured. "He will be so glad that I saved you. He will change his mind about you. He will change his mind about both of us..."

On the road back up to the palace that evening, Anna was in such a good mood that even the sight of Ivan, waiting impatiently for her on the palace steps, could not upset her.

Most days she did her best to avoid her brother. In such a large palace it was not hard to put distance between them, especially when she spent so much time at the stables or out in the grounds with Boris and Igor. Right now though avoidance was impossible. She gave her brother a weak smile as he towered over her – Ivan had grown considerably since his father's absence. "Hello, Brother."

"Hello, little sister," Ivan's grin was dark and nasty. "I have been growing very cold standing here waiting for you."

Anna tried not to glare at him. "Why were you waiting?"

"Do not be alarmed!" Ivan said. "I only wanted to give you a compliment. I wanted to tell you how nicely you ride."

Anna felt her heart stutter. "You saw me?"

"I was hunting pheasant down by the river," Ivan replied, as if she hadn't spoken. "And I looked up and there you were, mounted on a grey horse that I had never seen before. Is he new to the stables?"

Anna could not resist the pride swelling in her heart. "Ivan, that horse is the son of Smetanka! He is the finest horse in all of Russia!"

Ivan's mouth twisted in delight, and his grin became menacing. "Little sister, tsk tsk, what secrets you keep! So you have the son of Smetanka at the stables. And I'm guessing you have kept him alive against our father's orders? Oh, little sister, he's going to be furious when I tell him. He still hasn't forgiven you for killing his prize Arab, you know. Once he finds out that you kept Smetanka's ugly, useless offspring alive he will see to it that your horse is as dead as its sire!"

"You're a beast!" Anna spat the words at him. "You are the most heartless and cruel person I have ever met!"

"And you are far too sensitive," Ivan replied coolly. "But then you always were. I expect you will sob like a baby when father slits its throat…"

Anna flung herself at her brother, fists pounding at Ivan's chest until he shoved her away from him.

"Such a tantrum!" Ivan laughed at his sister. "I think I need to teach you a lesson…"

He grabbed her by the arm.

"*Niet!*" Anna cried. "Stop it! You're hurting me!"

She felt the blood rush to her face as her arm twisted up hard behind her back. She was struggling against Ivan, yelling at him to stop, in vain. And then, she saw the blur of orange-and-black fur streaking across the palace steps.

A tiger's roar at close range is the most terrifying

thing you will ever hear. Even Anna could not help but tremble at the sound. She saw her tiger leap to protect her from the boy who had once so viciously ripped out his whiskers. The young man who was now tormenting his mistress.

Ivan did not see Boris until the tiger was upon him. Dashed to the ground beneath the enormous weight of the big cat he released Anna instantly, and let out a blood-chilling scream. Anna, face down on the ground, turned over to see Boris straddling Ivan, crushing the boy beneath him. And then, with a growl of fury, the tiger lifted his mighty paw and struck the blow that changed their fates forever.

CHAPTER 9

The Madness of Ivan

Anna poked her head round the corner of Ivan's bedroom door.

"Can I come in?" she asked cautiously.

Ivan was sitting up in bed. He did not reply, but she entered his room anyway, tentatively walking to his bedside and sitting down in the nearby chair.

"I wanted to see how you were feeling, Brother," she said quietly.

"You mean you want to see what he did to me?" Ivan snarled. He turned his face round so that the right cheek was exposed. Anna could see a deep crimson incision that ran from temple to chin.

"Go on! Take a good look!"

Anna winced and turned away. "Ivan, I'm so sorry."

"Hah!" Ivan sneered. "You're not sorry yet. But you will be."

"What do you mean by that?"

"I mean I am ordering the serfs to have your tiger shot," Ivan said.

"Oh, please, Ivan, don't!" Anna felt her pulse racing. "He only attacked because he thought you were threatening me. He is very protective of me."

"Is he?" Ivan sneered. "Well, you will need to find a new protector. The tiger must be destroyed!"

"For goodness' sake, he only scratched you, Ivan! He could have killed you but he didn't!"

Ivan's face grew purple with rage.

For although the tiger had claws powerful enough to kill, the cut he had made was only skin deep. Boris had held back; he had only scratched Ivan to warn him away from hurting his mistress. All the same, it had been enough to cause Ivan to scream like a baby. When the housekeepers who had gathered at the commotion began to beat the tiger with brooms, Boris gave another roar of fury, as if to say, "Leave me alone! He started it!" Then he leapt off the young man and bounded away, heading out through the gardens, past animals screeching wildly in their gilded cages as he ran by.

On the palace steps, the housekeepers shouted at each other as they scrambled to help the young Lord Orlov.

"Give him room to breathe!" Katia pushed them all away. Ivan was still screaming, his hands clutching at his face. Anna saw Katia's look of horror, and then she heard the head housemaid exclaim under her breath. Two words, spoken in French, which Anna had heard many times before.

"*Le Balafre.*"

***

Anna ran down the wide corridors of the palace to her bedroom. From her wardrobe she pulled out her thick silver fur coat, fur hat and fur-lined boots and hurriedly got dressed. Then she ran through the corridors once more and headed out across the front steps and down the long winding driveway that led to the stables.

"What are you doing, Lady Anna?" Vasily asked when he found her in Drakon's stall, saddling up the grey stallion.

"I have to go," Anna told him. "Ivan is going to have Boris killed! I have to make sure that he gets as far away from the palace as possible!"

"Where will you go?"

"The forests of the taiga," Anna replied.

"It is too dangerous! There are tigers and all manner of wild creatures out there." Vasily looked worried.

"And that is the point!" Anna said as she put her foot in the stirrup and leapt up on to Drakon's back. "It is time for Boris to go home."

***

It was snowing. The flakes fell lightly at first, tiny stars shimmering like crystals on the collar of her fur coat, tingling against the warm skin of her cheeks. As Anna reached the great gates that led out of the

Khrenovsky estate, without a sound Boris fell in step with her stallion.

Igor panted alongside them. Anna had tried to stop the borzoi from joining the expedition; had entreated him to go back home, but Igor was not about to be left out from an adventure. He could not have known how this fateful journey was going to end. Or perhaps he did know – because strangely that day, instead of racing ahead and circling back again, the hound stayed close to Anna, Drakon and Boris the whole time, trotting along next to the tiger, as if he knew that this would be their last journey together.

In the grey skies above, the hooded crows circled, following the curious party: girl, horse, hound and tiger. Anna imagined the world from their lofty perspective, looking down at the three indistinct specks making their way doggedly across the white terrain. The taiga stretched out ahead of them. Only a few fir trees dotted the horizon – the world out here was a bleak wasteland.

"Come on." Anna coaxed Drakon into a trot. "We need to get moving. Ivan will soon realise that we are gone and he will send a hunting party after us. We need to make speed, Drakon. We must get Boris to safety."

It was not just Boris that she feared for. Her father was due back home within the month and when he knew that she had kept Smetanka's colt alive against his will, then Drakon's life would be in danger too. Anna had briefly considered letting the stallion go free along with the tiger, but in her heart she knew that Drakon could not possibly survive out here alone. Even though he was hardier than his father, Smetanka, being let loose in the wild in the middle of winter would kill him. That was if the timber wolves didn't get him first. Anna shuddered to think of the dead-eyed, baleful predators that stalked through the woods. No, her horse would have to come back with her to the Khrenovsky estate. They would have to take their chances and face Count Orlov together. This last journey across the taiga was for Boris alone.

As Drakon's trot became faster and faster, Boris began to lope in a graceful stride to keep pace and Anna felt her heart break. It had always been one of her greatest joys to watch the beautiful tiger's stripes rippling in motion, vibrating with the raw energy of his muscles undulating beneath the fur.

She felt her breath choke in her chest as she thought about never seeing him again. Yet the last thing Boris needed was for her to cry like a baby. Anna wiped the tears roughly from her frozen cheeks and rode on. She could not change the past. There was nothing to do except keep riding into the vast wasteland that lay beyond the estate.

It seemed like they had been riding forever. Drakon maintained his rhythm but Anna could see that the borzoi was struggling to keep pace with the stallion. Boris was tiring too, but still she drove her horse on. They desperately needed to get a head start on Ivan's men and run far enough away to make it impossible for them to track the tiger.

When the forest rose up before them, Anna knew that they had done it. The pawprints that they had left behind them in the white powder would be all but erased by the falling snow in an hour or two. And now that they were in the trees it would be impossible for the hunting party to find an animal as skilled at camouflage as Boris was. They could stop running now.

And yet Anna didn't stop. Because if she halted Drakon and brought their journey to an end then this was really happening. If they stopped she would have to say goodbye.

"Just a little further," she told her horse. "We should take Boris deep into the forest and then we will know he is safe."

Finally, as the skies darkened, she found herself deep within the gloomy wood and an open glade appeared before her, a barren circle in the midst of the thick woods that was clear of trees. Here, the snow had not yet smothered the mossy ground completely, and there were still pockets of verdant green showing through the patches of winter drift. Anna dismounted and stood in the eerie silence of the forest. There were no bird cries here, only the whisper of the snow falling on the boughs, and the growling purr of the big cat standing resolutely at her side.

Anna dropped to her knees and put her face right

up in front of Boris. His jaws were open wide as he panted. He was exhausted. They had run as far as they could.

"So," she said softly. "We have come far enough, I hope. It is time, Boris."

The tiger, still growling his big cat purr, shut his amber eyes and Anna did the same. She could feel his warm kitteny breath on her face. She leant forward and she kissed the tip of his pink nose.

"Borenka." Her eyes shone with tears. "You know that I love you. So you must know that I do not do this because I want to. It is because I have to. My brother Ivan will kill you if he finds you. This is the only way to keep you safe."

The tiger looked at her, still purring, and at that moment she felt as if he were saying: "It's all right, I understand."

"You will be fine." Anna was trying to reassure her tiger and also herself. "I know it. Your parents Veronika and Valery, they were wild once. Now I am returning you to the forests that they came from. This is your true home, Boris. Not some gilt palace with a borzoi and a horse for friends. Here, you will

155

meet a tiger mate, you will have cubs of your own. You will hunt and run and grow old and live a real life."

There were tears running down Anna's cheeks and her voice was trembling.

"I am setting you free, Borenka. Igor and Drakon and me, we are going back to Khrenovsky, but you alone, you must stay. Can you do that for me?"

The tiger's purr changed to a disgruntled growl and Anna's heart broke just that little bit more. "Boris, please!"

The tiger growled again, but this time he lay down. His great head rested in resignation on his front paws, and his tail, normally so twitchy and busy, was completely still. He understood. He would stay.

Anna dashed the tears from her eyes once more and mounted Drakon. The horse whinnied in disagreement, but Anna was firm with him and turned him back towards the estate. Igor whimpered and dragged his heels, but he did not disobey. The wolfhound fell in beside Drakon and walked slowly by the grey stallion with his head hanging low. Anna bit her lip, fighting back yet more tears. And then, unable to resist the urge, she looked back over her shoulder to have one last glimpse of the tiger that she so dearly loved.

But the clearing was empty. There was nothing but a tiger-shaped imprint in the snow.

***

Ivan's search party returned home from their hunt empty-handed – unable to find Anna's beloved beast in the wilderness. Anna knew that she had saved Boris's life, but her heartache in missing him was so profound that she wept for him every night as she fell asleep. She spent the weeks that followed riding the perimeter of the estate with Drakon and Igor. She told Vasily that this was part of Drakon's training, that she was teaching the grey stallion how to be a carriage horse. It was true that she was schooling him to accept the harness and to run with the weight of the carriage strapped to him. But she was also keeping a vigil, looking out for signs of her tiger. Her heart desperately wanted

Boris to come back so that she might see him just one more time, but her head knew better. If Boris was to live then he must stay away from Khrenovsky forever.

*

Almost a month later, Anna was out on one of her tours that took her as far as the gates of the estate. The grey stallion was just as swift under harness as he was when she rode him with a saddle. Winter had fully arrived and the carriage threw up great gouts of white as they sped across the fields. Igor, who had become spoilt like an only child since Boris was no longer around, was not running alongside the carriage. Instead, he had taken up a comfortable position nestled in the luggage space at Anna's feet under the bargeboard. Vasily had come with her in the carriage so that she could show him how marvellously well Drakon's training was progressing. Anna had to admit that it was also nice to have a companion to talk with for once.

"Do you know what is going on at the palace?"

Anna asked the groom. "I have seen the serfs busying themselves like crazy in the kitchens. There was a wild boar brought in yesterday and a fell deer. And the housemaids are putting flowers everywhere and the windows are being cleaned and the floors are polished to a high sheen. I asked Katia what was going on and she was flustered and said that Father was due home with guests."

"We have been asked to prepare thirty stable boxes for their horses," Vasily said. "It must be a large party."

"All the same…" Anna frowned. "He has brought visitors to the estate before without such preparation…"

Her words trailed off. There was a rumbling noise, growing louder by the second. The sound of many horses' hooves pounding on the roads. She looked up and saw a large party approaching the wide-open gates of the estate.

"Vasily! Look!" Most of the riders were on horseback, but there was also a *cortège* with three riders on guard, surrounding a very grand, gilt-trimmed enclosed carriage. The royal insignia had been painted on its sides and six gorgeous horses dressed in the finest livery towed it.

"If I am not mistaken," Vasily said as he dropped into a deep bow. "That is the carriage of the Empress herself!"

Anna stiffened in awe. Her father had brought the Empress home with him!

"What do I do?" she hissed to Vasily as she dropped into a hasty curtsey.

"You are asking me?" Vasily said. "Lady Anna, I am not the person to give directions on the etiquette of meeting royalty!"

"There is Father!" Anna saw Count Orlov riding at the front of the party. He sat astride a magnificent black horse, with another rider on a matching horse of equal beauty riding alongside him. Behind these two horses came the royal carriage, flanked by its mounted guards. Anna's eyes were glued on the carriage as the party drew closer. The golden silk curtains were drawn tightly closed, though she was hoping that she might see a gloved hand reach up and pull them apart so that she could get a glimpse inside. A chance to see the Empress herself at last!

"Anna." The Count greeted his daughter as he pulled up his horse in front of her carriage. "You have grown, my girl."

"Yes, she has," agreed the rider alongside him, who was wearing a green uniform. "She looks so much like her mother. Countess Orlov was one of the greatest beauties of the royal court in her day."

Anna glanced across at the rider sitting astride the big black horse beside Count Orlov. She had been too busy looking at the magnificent royal carriage to notice that the rider was not a man, but a woman, dressed in military garb, riding astride in jodhpurs and long boots with a sword and a fur hat. The woman was elegant and grey-haired and she had an energy around her that seemed to overshadow even Count Orlov's presence.

Empress Catherine of Russia.

Anna turned to redirect her clumsy curtsey, bumping herself on the bargeboard as she did so.

"Forgive me for not recognising you straight away, Your Royal Highness," she managed to stutter. "I thought you were riding in the carriage!"

The Empress wheeled her horse about and sat up

tall in the saddle. "I cannot abide long journeys cooped in there," she said. "My dogs and my maids-in-waiting are in the carriage but I prefer to ride a horse myself."

"Yes, me too!" Anna smiled, then quickly added, "Your Majesty."

The Empress laughed. "And is this your own horse, the one you have harnessed to this carriage? He looks a very unusual sort. One of your father's wonderful experiments, I assume?"

Anna felt her stomach drop. Until this moment her father had never seen Drakon. The Count was not yet aware that his wishes had been defied and that Smetanka's doomed foal was still alive. There had been a vague chance that in the commotion of the royal arrival Anna could have hidden the stallion from him once more, but now the Empress had directly drawn attention to Drakon. There was no escaping fate.

"This is the son of my father's foundation sire, the great Arab stallion Smetanka." Anna tried to keep the tremble out of her voice as she saw her father's face darken. "His name is Drakon and he is the fastest horse in all of Russia under harness."

"The fastest horse in all of Russia!" Empress

Catherine laughed. "Well, your father certainly has a gift for breeding the very best."

She turned to the Count. "Do you hold this horse in as high a regard as your daughter does?"

Count Orlov was silent for a moment. Even during his fury, Anna could see his masterful eye at work. He was examining Drakon's long back, the strong legs, the dinner-plate-sized hooves that would grip even the slipperiest surface of a frozen lake.

"I was not impressed with him as a colt," the Count said. "Yet I see that perhaps he has grown into something more pleasing. I should like to see him run. I reserve my judgement on him until then. Perhaps he might suit my breeding programme, if he shows stamina. But…" He paused, staring at Anna. "I am always prepared for disappointment."

Empress Catherine laughed. "No one would be foolish enough to disappoint you, Count Orlov!" she teased him gaily. Then she turned back to Anna. "I look forward to spending more time with you, child, at the ball tonight. I was a great friend of your mother's and I think you and I shall become close companions."

"Anna is not coming to the royal ball," Count Orlov said stiffly.

"Well, of course she is!" The Empress spoke firmly. "Take care not to refuse my wishes in future, Alexei."

Count Orlov quickly hid the emotion from his face and bowed deeply. "As you wish, Majesty, the child will attend."

"Excellent!" The Empress dusted the snow from her shoulders with a fur-gloved hand. "Now come, let us ride on! I am assuming the palace is not far from here. I am Empress and I think the time has come for me to be treated as such. I want a banquet prepared and rose petals soaking in my bathtub by the time I am ready to dismount from my horse. See to it, Alexei."

And with that, the Empress turned down the road towards the Khrenovsky estate at a brisk trot. Count Orlov had no choice but to spur his own horse on ahead to prepare the palace for their arrival. Empress Catherine the Great had spoken.

***

As Anna sat at her dressing table to begin her *toilette* she felt like she was floating on the music of the string orchestra playing downstairs. Outside her bedroom she could hear the polite chatter of the guests as they made their way downstairs. Soon the dancing would begin. Then the Empress would arrive and the guests would queue to be received, curtseying and bowing before their sovereign in the grand ballroom.

Katia had laid out Anna's most beautiful gown on the bed. It was her favourite, silver satin, with pretty filigree lace at the chest. Anna admired her reflection in the mirror, dusting her *décolletage* with powder, rouging the apples of her cheeks and adding a beauty spot with kohl pencil. That was an old-fashioned affectation, but she knew her mother would have approved. Lastly, she reached down to the jewellery box in front of her, withdrew the black diamond necklace and held it up to her throat.

As the cold teardrop jewel touched her warm skin she felt lightning run through her. She looked up once more at her reflection in the mirror as she did up the silver clasp. Holding her breath, she shut her eyes and clutched the gemstone tight in her hands. And then, as the vision overtook her, she was no longer in the palace. The diamond had possessed her once more.

CHAPTER 10

Flying Changes

Circus life had been gruelling, but it was nothing compared to how hard Valentina worked at the Academy. Her day started at 5am. There were sixteen massive warmbloods to feed, and by the time she had lugged hay to their loose boxes, filled their water troughs and mixed their oats and maize, it was dawn and she was starving. Breakfast was served up at the main house and the riders, Natalia and Olga, and Oscar and Molly along with George Mueller and the twins' mother, Ingrid, would sit down at the table and discuss the day's programme. Valentina would heap her plate with *blini* and salmon and winter berries and listen

167

carefully while George Mueller briefed her on which horses to prepare.

By 7am Valentina would be back at the stables, mucking out the loose boxes and tacking up the first four horses for Natalia, Olga and the twins.

"Their saddles must always be polished, manes pulled and legs bandaged," George Mueller explained. "I expect my horses to look as good in the *ménage* as they do when they are out competing."

If a horse was young and green, then Valentina would take it into the arena to work on the lunge rein. The side reins and chambon for this task were the same as she had used to train Sasha for vaulting. She knew how to use a whip to send the horse out and make it circle her at the end of the rope in a steady stride as she relied on voice commands to make it walk, trot and canter.

Once a horse had begun to stretch and use its body like an athlete, she would uncouple it from the lunge gear and get it ready for its rider.

At 8am the training sessions would begin. Standing in the shadows, Valentina watched and absorbed everything. She didn't know the fancy names for the movements – the pirouettes and piaffes and half-passes, but she understood how to make them happen, as clearly as if she were riding the horses herself.

In the circus the trick was to make it look as if the horse was doing all the work and the rider was doing nothing, as if the movements happened by magic. These dressage riders did the same thing, relying on the smallest shift in their balance or the subtlest squeeze of their legs to send their horses flying around the arena. This dressage was new to her, but the art of camouflage, of keeping the sleight of hand hidden from the audience, was something she had been training for her whole life.

Valentina loved to watch George Mueller as he coached his riders. The old man with ice-white hair and the leathery tan that came from spending a lifetime outdoors could easily have been sixty years old. Yet his posture was erect and his gait was lively and spry. He possessed the same lean build as his niece and nephew, and he dressed smartly in beige jodhpurs, long bronze leather riding boots and the same short-sleeved, collared polo shirt that his riders wore – with the eagle insignia of the Russian Federation and his name across the back in large capital letters.

The head coach was an unflinching taskmaster, pushing his riders to the limit of their stamina and skills. Valentina marvelled at his instinct and sense of timing with the horses. "Try to carry your hands a little higher and I think you may find your half-passes would be straighter," he would advise Natalia. And then to Olga, "Do not tilt to the left when you ask for a flying change."

Natalia, an ex-ballerina, took his criticism with a smile, and so did Oscar and Molly. But Olga did not like to be told what to do and their training sessions often ended with her in a foul mood.

One day when Valentina was leading a new horse into the arena for Olga, she got stuck in the middle of a heated exchange.

"I am not riding this horse any more. He is no good." Olga stood with her hands on her hips, refusing to get on board. "Why won't you buy me decent horses?"

"Olga." George Mueller's voice was calm. "Raffy cost the country a million euro…"

"Pah!" Olga was unimpressed. "A good dressage horse, like the ones the Dutch and the Germans have, will cost at least ten million!"

"Russia cannot afford ten-million-euro horses!" the head coach countered.

"Russia cannot afford to lose its best dressage rider either!" Olga shot back. "The World Games in Stockholm are six months away and we have no horses and no game plan!"

"You should not speak like that to Herr Mueller! Raffy is an excellent horse but you don't listen!"

Valentina gasped as the words left her mouth and everyone turned to stare at her. Olga, who had already been furious, was now hysterical with rage.

"And what would you know about it, Miss Moscow Spectacular?" Olga's voice was shrill. "You think because you know how to ride circus tricks that you have any idea what it means to ride Grand Prix dressage?"

It was far too late to take her words back now so Valentina stood her ground. "I may not have ridden in the Grand Prix but my Sasha is a very nice mover. I trained him so I can cartwheel off his back at a canter. I think I can teach him to do a pirouette too."

Olga gave a hollow laugh. "A pink horse in the Grand Prix? That would not be ridiculous or anything!"

"Olga," George Mueller intervened. "That is enough. Mount up, please, and let us get started."

"Niet!" Olga stubbornly refused again. "I am not going to ride this rubbish any more. Get this groom on board her circus pony instead – maybe she can ride him to the Olympics!"

Valentina watched as Olga stormed off, and then she turned to George Mueller.

"I am sorry," she apologised. "I shouldn't have spoken out like that."

"Don't worry, Valentina." George Mueller shook his head in wry amusement. "With Olga it is always that the horses are not good enough. It is never her riding that is at fault!"

George Mueller put a hand on Raffy's shoulder. "She will be back, but not today. Put Raffy on the lunge instead and then put him back in his loose box, all right?"

"All right," Valentina smiled.

*

Natalia had to ride all of Olga's horses as well as her own that day and so the training took a little longer than usual. It was almost eight o'clock by the time Valentina was doing the last of the evening feeds. Natalia stayed back to help her out.

"You should not be doing this work," Valentina said.

"I don't mind." Natalia smiled and dug her pitchfork into the hay. "You are the best groom we have ever had, Valentina. Don't let Olga get to you. She was exactly the same with me when I came here."

Valentina frowned. "All the time it is the same. The horses are never good enough for her."

"Olga is from a very wealthy family," Natalia replied. "She's had top-class horses since she was six years old. People like her in the dressage world, they are obsessed with bloodlines. And then you turn up from the circus with Sasha, this bizarre creature…"

Natalia saw the look on Valentina's face. "Oh, I did not mean to offend," she added hastily. "It is not what I think, Valentina! I love Sasha. He is so cute with his funny pink colour. But there are a lot of snobs in this sport, you know? All the time with them it must be fancy warmbloods. What I am saying is, don't let it upset you."

Natalia threw the last of the hay into the feed bins. "Are you coming up to the house for dinner then?"

"In a little while," Valentina replied. "I have some more things to do here."

Valentina checked all the horses, making sure they were bandaged and comfortable for the night before she returned to Sasha's stall. The pink horse had his head over the door to greet her.

"Don't worry, Sasha, I think you are the most beautiful horse in the world," Valentina told him. The stallion responded by burrowing his head into her chest, using her as a scratching post.

"Come on." Valentina opened the stable door, flung the numnah on to his back and slid the saddle on top. "It's playtime."

***

At this hour there was never anyone in the *ménage*. Natalia, Olga and the twins were having dinner at the house. The lights had been turned out, but Valentina switched them on again and the three central ceiling domes above the sand flickered to life.

Sasha had been in his stall since the morning and he gave deep snorts, clearing his nostrils as Valentina let him walk out on a loose rein to get his shoulders moving. Then she began to do stretches of her own in the saddle, limbering up as she raised her arms above her head and bent them down her back.

She moved into a trot and Sasha carried himself elegantly, head tucked low, hocks moving beneath him. Valentina clucked him on and pressed her leg on to the left and Sasha began to cross his legs over and dance sideways in a smooth leg yield. She put her right leg on and the pink horse danced back the other way.

Valentina came down the long side of the arena in a canter, keeping her gaze high, her shoulders back, her hands held aloft. At the corner, with the precision of a racing-car driver on a hairpin bend, she used a half-halt to prepare Sasha, sitting him back on his hocks. Then she rounded the corner and felt the music in her head surge as she asked him to skip, left-leg-right-leg-left-leg. And then they were on the other side of the arena and she was holding him up with his poll high and pushing him forward into the extended canter strides so that he swept across the sand. Still she did not let him go; she held herself like she was carrying a tray of champagne in her hands, a phrase that George Mueller often used. She rode every single moment with no smile on her face; nothing but the mask of pure concentration.

When she felt that every sinew and muscle of Sasha was attuned to her seat and legs and hands, she asked her horse to elevate and trot on the spot. Suddenly his hindquarters became a mighty engine beneath her, and Sasha arched his neck like the fiercest stallion, and they were in piaffe! The raw energy that had served him so well in the circus was just as powerful in the *ménage*. Only now with Valentina's legs wrapped round him and her hands held high, he piaffed beneath her just like a Grand Prix stallion!

And yet here under the floodlights of the academy there was not a single soul to see it. No cheering crowd. No buffooning clowns. No surly ringmaster. She was all alone.

Valentina threw her arms round Sasha, giving him a giant hug. "I don't care if no one saw that, Sasha. You are such a star," she breathed into his mane.

"Valentina!"

She looked up to see George Mueller striding across the arena towards her.

"We must talk," he said.

"I am sorry, Herr Mueller…" Valentina stammered. "I shouldn't have switched the lights back on. I know I am not supposed to be riding…"

"Valentina." George Mueller shook his head. "Stop – you are not in trouble!"

"I'm not?"

The head coach paused before he spoke again. "I have been watching you this evening," he said. "You have been doing these sessions with this horse often?"

Valentina nodded and blushed guiltily. "Most nights, when everyone else has gone to bed. Then I ride."

"So you taught him by yourself to piaffe like that?"

Valentina nodded.

George Mueller patted Sasha on his shoulder and looked up at the girl on his back. "Hmmm, yes... six months. If I begin to work with you now, it is enough time, I think."

"I don't understand," Valentina frowned.

"The way your horse trots, it is extraordinary," George Mueller said. "He has a long back and yet he is very collected. When you did the spin, the pirouette, he was placing his hind legs in perfect order. I would give him an eight for that in a Grand Prix test. And his piaffe! The cadence is excellent, his knees are high. A dressage judge would give him good marks for such a display. Very good marks..."

George Mueller stroked Sasha's pink muzzle. "This horse is going to be one of the greats. He will surprise everyone. That is, if you are willing to put in the hard work."

Valentina was stunned. "Do you mean you are going to let me ride?"

George Mueller stuck out his hand for her to shake. "Welcome aboard, Valentina Romanov. You are the newest member of the Russian Federation international team."

***

That night as Valentina lay in bed she had closed her fist tight round the black gemstone of her necklace. In an instant, she saw herself mounted up on Sasha's back in the grandest arena she had ever seen: pristine white sand under sparkling lights, edged with white boxes filled with blooming flowers, and an enormous crowd cheering as she took a bow. And at that moment she sensed the tension in the stallion beneath her and knew he might explode at any moment. He was relying on Valentina to hold him steady.

She put her fingers to her neck and there it was – her precious necklace. The anchor that held them both. Her heart raced as she clung tight to the stone and Valentina knew that she was seeing her destiny.

CHAPTER 11

The Grand Ball

Anna's visions of the pink stallion began to fade. She clutched the diamond tight in her fist and screwed her eyes shut. And when she opened them again she saw her mother's face reflected in the mirror.

The Countess was at the dressing table doing her make-up, and Anna was on her velvet cushion sitting cross-legged, watching her mother with wide eyes. She was laughing, telling stories, and in every movement and gesture, Anna saw the softness of her eyes and the kindness of her smile.

Then Anna's skin prickled with goosebumps as if the windows had been flung open wide in mid-winter.

They were not alone. There was somebody watching them, a shadowy figure standing in the doorway of the bedroom, glowering at them, black eyes seething from beneath a mop of dark hair.

Ivan!

Anna rose up from her velvet cushion and smiled at her brother, beckoning Ivan to join them, but he didn't move. The dark expression on her brother's face twisted with jealousy and his hands clenched angrily. And, unseen by their mother, Ivan mouthed at Anna these words: "I will *always* hate you, little sister."

Anna was crying, tears hot and wet on her cheeks. She had always thought that her brother hated her for no reason at all, but now she saw that he was jealous and always would be. Not even the terrible loss of their mother could change him.

Anna opened her eyes and released her grip on the stone, gasping for breath. Her cheeks were still hot and wet with tears, and she wiped them roughly with her hand. Too late she realised she had smeared the make-up she had just so carefully applied. She would have to start again...

"Hello, Sister."

Standing right behind her in the doorway was Ivan.

Igor, who had been lying silently at Anna's feet, stood up and let out a low, menacing growl.

"Are you ready to make your entrance?" Ivan asked. "Father says I am to accompany you into the ballroom."

"I…"Anna hesitated. "I need just a few minutes, to correct my make-up…"

Ivan stood impassive in the doorway. "Go on, then," he said. "Do it."

Anna powdered over her cheeks once more with trembling hands, while Ivan smouldered with rage at her, just as he had done all those years ago. Hurriedly she reapplied the beauty spot and daubed crimson on her lips. She stood up and Igor brushed against her skirts expectantly.

"*Niet*. You wait for me here, Igor," Anna instructed. "A ball is no place for a hound."

She smoothed her dress and took a deep breath.

"I'm ready," she said.

***

The grand ballroom was filled with colour, the ladies in frilly satin gowns of every shade imaginable, with feathers decorating their hair. They fluttered their fans theatrically, ducking behind them to whisper to one another, greeting their friends with self-conscious smiles, while their husbands stood beside them, stiff and formal in their dinner suits. All the crowd seemed desperately aware that they were soon to be in the presence of Empress Catherine the Great.

"Come on then!" Ivan said impatiently, urging Anna to the top of the stairs where a gold-liveried footman waited. "The Lord Ivan and the Lady Anna of Khrenovsky," he announced as brother and sister stepped forward together. Ivan gave Anna a distinctly fake smile as he put out his arm. She placed her fingertips upon it and they descended the stairs to join the party.

Anna had never felt so uncomfortable in all her life. As she took step after step in her high heels she tightened her grip on Ivan's arm. It was all so frightfully grown-up!

"Stop pinching me – we are here now!" Ivan hissed as soon as they had descended the final step.

He yanked his arm away and strode to the centre of the room. Anna watched his brazen confidence as he pushed his way towards a giggling group of young Countesses.

In the midst of all this gaiety and frivolity Ivan's darkness made him a compelling figure. He had witnessed from early childhood how the Count had played upon his disfigurement as *Le Balafre*. Now Ivan did the same thing, brandishing his own scar like a badge of courage.

"Did you know he earned it fighting a tiger bare-handed?" Anna heard one of the ladies telling her friend as they promenaded past Anna, whispering into their fans.

"Really?" her friend exclaimed. "He must be very brave indeed to fight such a fierce beast!"

"Oh yes! He is the bravest man in all of Russia," the first young lady replied. "And a great horseman just like his father."

Anna listened to their exchange in disbelief. Ivan, meanwhile, was still manoeuvring his way through the crowds, moving ever closer to the Empress.

For Empress Catherine was already seated at the

far end of the ballroom, on a golden throne that had been placed directly beneath the crystal chandelier. Flanking her were her most loyal and important nobles. Count Orlov stood directly to the left of her throne, dressed in his military regalia with a pale blue cummerbund bound round his waist. On the other side of the Empress was Anna's uncle Grigory. Anna noticed how he would whisper conspiratorially to the Empress in a manner that made Anna blush.

Into this group of dignitaries strode Ivan. He marched straight up to the Empress, and after the curtest of bows began to address Her Royal Highness directly. Anna noted a flicker of annoyance on Empress Catherine's face, but Ivan didn't seem to care. He kept talking and talking until eventually the monarch whispered to one of her aides. The footman immediately stepped in and ushered Ivan away.

Anna did not dare approach the throne herself. She found an alcove behind the chamber orchestra where there was an unoccupied *chaise longue* and she sat there, happy to be hidden and yet right in the midst of the gaiety. She loved watching the courtiers dancing and laughing. The orchestra was playing waltzes and the Empress rose to dance with Count Orlov.

Anna watched the way her father held the Empress lightly at the waist as they waltzed, and how she laughed and smiled at his conversation. The dance had only just finished when from across the dance floor a man with a thick black beard and black eyes approached them.

"May I have the pleasure of the next dance, Your Majesty?" he asked.

"Count Smirnov!" the Empress exclaimed, "What a delight to see you here. How was your journey? It must have been exhausting to come so very far."

Count Smirnov bowed deeply. "I would go to the ends of the earth to dance with Your Majesty!"

Count Orlov harrumphed at Count Smirnov's attempts to charm, but if the Empress noticed she hid it well.

"I was just speaking with Count Orlov," she said, "about his marvellous new carriage trotter. Did you know he believes that he has bred the greatest stallion in all of Russia?"

Anna's heart pounded in her chest. Were they talking about Drakon?

Count Smirnov's eyes widened and then he gave an uncomfortable, forced laugh.

"Your Majesty, Count Orlov is undoubtedly an excellent breeder of hounds and chickens and various rare oddities, but surely he cannot claim to breed the best carriage horses? My Kabarda stallion is certainly the finest and the fastest in all of Russia."

Around the room, the tinkling of laughter and the conversation quieted as the other guests caught wind of the conversation between the two Counts and their Empress.

"If you wish to see the finest stallion in all of Russia, Count Orlov —" Count Smirnov intoned – "then visit your stables, for I have brought him here with me! My Kabarda stallion is unsurpassed!"

"Hah! I do not think so!" A voice rang out across the ballroom and a gentleman dressed in a purple satin cummerbund stepped forward to join the Empress's group.

"Your Majesty," Count Petrov bowed stiffly. "Count Smirnov is surely not saying that he possesses the perfect carriage horse? Everyone knows that my Turkmene stallion is by far superior. And I too have my horse stabled at Khrenovsky…"

At that point the entire ballroom erupted into argument. It seemed that there were at least a dozen nobles present who believed that their horse was superior to all others.

As the throng gathered around her and the bickering became fevered and tense, the Empress stayed serene. She stood with an expression of unabashed amusement as the nobles got more and more agitated. Each man raised his voice louder, trying to drown out all others. And then, without saying a word, the Empress raised the goblet that she had been drinking from, and tapped a fork lightly against the glass, ringing out a chime that silenced all of them.

"There!" she smiled. "That is better. Such passions you all have! Clearly we must settle this once and for all."

"As you say, Your Majesty," Count Smirnov

agreed. "If you would like to inspect the horses at the stables…"

"Oh no!" The Empress laughed. "Count Smirnov, you claim that you possess the fastest carriage horse in Russia. And such a boast can only be settled in one way…"

The Empress took in the entire ballroom with her regal gaze and then proclaimed, "We shall have a race tomorrow."

A murmur of excitement rippled through the crowd.

"Your Majesty is indeed wise!" Count Smirnov said. "A race across the black ice of the River Voronezh will settle this!"

Count Petrov snorted. "The Voronezh? Pah! A sprint along the river proves nothing. Stamina is the true worth of a horse. Let the race be held across the vast distances of the taiga!"

There were more shouts and disagreement but the assembled guests fell silent as the Empress spoke once more.

"We shall do both," she said, smiling. "The race will begin on the river ice and then it will continue across the taiga. The horses will run all the way to the Bridge of the Single Pine and then back again to the Khrenovsky estate."

She turned to Count Orlov. "Every man who thinks his horse can outrun your trotter shall have his chance to prove it!"

Count Orlov was about to speak, but before he had the chance, Ivan stepped forward.

"I should be honoured to race our horse for you, Father."

"Well spoken, Ivan." Count Orlov looked at his son proudly. "My son shall take the reins of my new stallion."

"No!"

Until this moment Anna had been a silent spectator, biting her tongue as the men all boasted and bragged about their horses. But the idea that Ivan should take the reins of her beloved Drakon? It was simply too much for her.

"He is not yours to race!" Anna shouted. "He is my horse. I saved him from the executioner's blade. I cared for him as a foal, raised him as a colt and broke him to saddle and harness. Drakon is mine and if anyone is going to race him in this contest it should be me!"

Count Orlov's face was dark with fury. "Do not be ridiculous, Anna!" he growled. "The open taiga is no place for a woman…"

As soon as he said the words, he visibly regretted them. The room took on a distinctly chilly air as everyone turned to the Empress. She held the silence until it became almost painful, and then frostily said, "So a woman cannot race a carriage horse, Count Orlov? And yet, as you see, a woman is capable of ruling the whole of Russia. Or perhaps you think a man would be better in my place too?"

Count Orlov spluttered and stammered.

"Forgive me, Your Majesty. I only meant that my son was older. Anna is but a girl, she is only thirteen."

Empress Catherine's face was stony with displeasure. "Count Orlov, you do your daughter a great disservice. She is young, but she is clearly capable, aren't you, child?"

A hundred guests filled the grand ballroom at Khrenovsky and right now all of them were looking at Anna, waiting for her to speak. She could feel her heart racing, her mouth dry and her breath choking in her throat.

"Please, Your Majesty. I know I am only a girl, but I am as brave as any man. I want to race my stallion. I am not afraid."

The Empress clapped her hands together with delight.

"Darling girl!" She said. "Such courage! You remind me so much of myself at your age. Of course you must be the one to race your horse. Alexei, you will make it so."

The Empress turned away from Count Orlov and addressed the assembled nobles. "Let all those who wish to compete gather at dawn on the Western Lawn. We shall discover tomorrow which horse is the greatest in all of my realm."

***

It was well after midnight when the ball came to an end. Anna, who had never stayed up so late at night before, and who had danced until her feet were sore, was exhausted. She had made her way back to her bedroom and was about to get changed into her nightgown when Ivan appeared once more at her door.

"Hello, Sister," he said.

She spun round, startled. "Ivan! I looked for you at the ball. I wanted to talk to you but I couldn't find you," Anna said. "I am sorry, I didn't mean to embarrass you…"

"Embarrass me?" Ivan laughed bitterly. "We shall see who looks a fool when tomorrow comes!"

Igor, who had been resting at the foot of the bed, began to growl, and came to stand protectively at Anna's side.

"What do you mean?" Anna asked.

Ivan gave a wicked grin. "Oh, nothing," he said airily. "I was just wondering; have you checked on your horse yet this evening?"

Anna was horrified. "Ivan! What have you done?" She did not wait for an answer. She grabbed her fur coat and ran.

The snow was falling heavily as she sprinted down the slippery marble stairs at the front entrance of the palace. She felt her feet nearly fly out from underneath her, but she managed to keep her footing. She ran all the way along the gravel path to the stables and did not stop until she had reached Drakon's stall.

"Drakon?" Her heart was racing. If Ivan had even touched her horse...

"Drakon!"

He was right there in his stall, his eyes bright, ears pricked.

"Oh, thank goodness!" She threw her arms round him. "I thought he had hurt you!"

There was an oil lamp burning low in the corner of the stables and she raised it aloft as she examined the grey stallion: checking his legs, looking in his feed bin, sniffing and then tasting the water in his trough. If Ivan had been trying to scare her, his tactic had certainly worked. Typical of her brother to play mind games with her!

She collapsed into the straw on the floor of Drakon's stall. The big grey horse walked over and lowered his enormous head so that his muzzle was right up against her face. His breath was sweet like meadow hay, a soft warm breeze against her ice-cold skin. It was freezing tonight. Already the snow had fallen heavily enough to deeply cover the palace lawn. Tomorrow the drifts would become treacherous. The course across the taiga would be terribly dangerous. But tonight all Anna could think of was her wonderful horse.

"You will not let me down, Drakon. You are not only the fastest but the most intelligent, the most loyal, the most courageous horse in the whole of Russia," she whispered to him. "And tomorrow, we will prove this in front of the Empress – and there will never again be talk of the executioner's axe for you."

Anna shivered, feeling the sting of the night air on her skin. It was too cold to linger – she had to get back inside the palace where it was warm.

"Goodnight, my dearest." She gave the horse one last kiss on his velvet muzzle and then left his stall, locking it behind her.

As she strode up the row, she passed the stalls of Drakon's opponents and eyed each of them in turn. She passed the stall of the Kabarda stallion, a dark bay with eyes as black and beady as those of his master. Beside him, the Turkmene stallion with a coat of burnished copper and long, lithe limbs was eating from his hay feeder. And next to him stood the horse of Count Sokolov, a skinny grey with a ewe neck.

If Anna had shifted her gaze from the stalls and looked in the opposite direction she would have seen the row of carriages, including her own, a pretty affair painted pink and turquoise, with gilt trim on the framework and burnished wooden wheels.

Even if she had taken the time to glance at the carriage frame, however, it is unlikely she would have noticed her brother's handiwork with the axe.

The cuts that Ivan had made when he sneaked out to the stables after the Empress's speech were well-hidden beneath the chassis. You would need to get down on bended knee and look underneath the carriage to see where his blows had gouged the rod of the axle.

Ivan's sabotage was masterful. The carriage would not collapse straight away. Anna and Drakon would start the race and at first the axle would hold. In fact, it should stay intact right up until they reached the rugged outlands. Only there, where the ground became hard and rocky, would the axle give at last, and the little sister who Ivan hated so much would be stranded miles from home and alone.

Ivan the Terrible would have his revenge at last.

CHAPTER 12

The Race

The next morning, Anna could not see out of her bedroom window. The ice was so thick it had crusted over the pane, and as the dawn light hit the frosty surface it turned a million tiny crystals into glistening gold.

As she dressed, Igor roused himself from the foot of her bed and made a great display of stretching and yawning. The borzoi stuck close at her heels as she walked the palace halls heading for the snow-covered lawn of the western wing. The carriage drivers and horses were already gathering outside.

Vasily was waiting, standing beside Drakon, the grey horse harnessed and prepared.

"A good morning for a race," Anna said, breathing mist into the air and rubbing her gloved hands together.

"*Niet*, Lady Anna," Vasily frowned. "Look at the clouds. A blizzard is coming…"

Anna's attention was drawn away by a commotion further down the lawn. Count Smirnov, dressed in a bearskin coat and hat with his bushy beard protruding from beneath it, looked almost like a wild animal himself as he struggled to control his Kabarda stallion, which was straining and lunging against the harness. The Count tried to subdue the stallion with his whip but the horse fought back with a squeal of fury, and struck out like a snake, his neck whiplashing, fangs bared. Count Smirnov began to rain blows upon his stallion and Anna, horrified at the sight of the horse being struck, turned away.

"That man is a beast!" she said through gritted teeth.

"There are worse than him," Vasily said, staring down the row of carriages at the Counts and Dukes now boarding and preparing to set off. "These men are battle-hardened. They have raced before, and you have not."

Anna clambered up into her carriage. "But I know the taiga better than any of them. And I have the best horse," she replied, trying to sound braver than she was truly feeling. She put out her hands for the reins. Reluctantly, Vasily passed them to her. "Promise me you will come home safe," he said.

Anna nodded. "I will."

The drivers were ready to depart. On the ground beside Anna's carriage Igor began to whimper loudly, begging to be allowed up to take his usual spot in the luggage hold.

"Not this time, Igor," Anna told him firmly. "The taiga is no place for you today."

The loud clang of a gong sounded and all eyes turned to the palace steps. The Empress appeared, dressed in a regal gown and a red velvet jacket with a high collar and matching hat trimmed with mink fur. Standing beside her, looking pleased to be presiding over the excitable crowd, was Count Orlov. A full head taller than the rest of the men present, he drew attention to his great height by wearing a silver turban plumed with peacock feathers. His dress was even more flamboyant than the Empress's – a full-length fur coat and beneath that a long silver and gold brocade robe, a glittering treasure that he had brought back from his travels in Turkey. He cast a look over the gathering as his serfs moved briskly through the crowds with silver trays of glasses.

The gong sounded again and silence fell as the Empress raised her goblet high in the air.

"My people," she smiled. "I am sure you all wish to thank Count Orlov for hosting us at his magnificent palace."

"A toast to Count Orlov!" one of the guests cried out.

"To Count Orlov!" The others chanted in unison as their goblets were thrust into the air and then emptied in a single gulp. The Empress raised her hand once more and silence fell.

"Count Orlov has told me often of his desire to create the ultimate Russian horse. He has made it his life's work here at Khrenovsky to produce the perfect carriage trotter – elegant, surefooted and swift enough to rival the greatest in all of Europe."

There was a murmur from the crowd. The Empress waited for silence before she continued. "Today we will see if the genius of Count Orlov is proven. His grey stallion, Drakon, son of the famous Smetanka, will be tested against the very best horses from the finest estates across our great nation.

"The race will run beyond the boundaries of this estate to the Bridge of the Single Pine. Here the drivers must fasten their heraldic colours and then return across the taiga to Khrenovsky Palace."

The Empress held out her goblet for a servant to refill it and then she lifted the vessel aloft once more. "Let us drink," she said, "to these thirteen valiant men…"

She corrected herself: "… *twelve* valiant men and one young girl. May the best horse in Russia win!"

"To the horses and to Russia!" Count Orlov reinforced the Empress's words as they all took great swigs.

Standing to the right of his father, dressed in a thick black fur, Ivan Orlov raised his goblet with the rest of them. His eyes met Anna's as he took a drink and he mouthed words to her: *Good luck, Sister.*

On the ground beside her carriage Igor, still whimpering, could stand it no longer. He leapt up and put his front paws on the carriage, trying to climb up beside Anna. Vasily had to grab hold of the hound and pull him back down again.

"Hang on to him and do not let go," Anna told Vasily. "Make sure he doesn't follow me."

The carriages began to move off. Anna gave Vasily and Igor an anxious smile as she tapped Drakon lightly on the rump with the whip. The grey stallion jolted forward and the carriage wheels began to roll as they took their place in the grand procession. The carriages moved in single file across the unmarked snow of the palace gardens, weaving between hedges and topiary, heading for the river.

As they rolled closer to the black, glassy surface of the Voronezh, Anna was feeling sick with nerves. She had not been on the river since that fateful day with Smetanka.

Anna held Drakon back and watched as the other carriage drivers guided their horses out on to the ice. These men with their stocky, thickset horses were much heavier than she and Drakon, Anna reasoned. If the ice could handle such burdens it would not crack beneath their slender weight.

"Come on, Drakon." She fought the sickness inside her, bracing herself as she asked the horse to take his first step out on to the ice.

Drakon did not hesitate. He walked out briskly, snorting in the icy morning air, plumes of steam coming from his nostrils. He set one hoof upon the ice and then the next and before Anna knew it they were on the river.

The cold wind whipped across the surface of the ice and swirled the snow in eddies around Anna, stinging her bare cheeks. She wished that her hat had ear flaps like Count Smirnov's. He had parked his carriage a little way away from her on the ice and now the other drivers were lining up their horses between them, forming a straight row across the river, preparing for the race to begin.

Through the icy, howling gale, Anna heard the nicker of horses and the groan of carriage wheels creaking. She thought about the cold, dark depths of the river directly below the ice. She had nearly died in the frozen waters that lay beneath her wheels.

She had never wanted to set foot on the ice again, but now she was here once more. With each anxious stamp of his hoof against the surface Drakon sent a shiver of fear down her spine. At that moment she wanted to turn back, to get off the black ice as fast as she could, but it was too late. The Empress had walked out on to the ice with Count Orlov, Ivan and a courtier carrying a gigantic blunderbuss. In her hand Her Majesty held aloft a red flag, which whipped and twisted in the wind as if it were trying to escape her grasp. As the riders tightened their grip on the reins, the Empress let the flag fly loose. It gusted up into the air and stayed there for a brief moment, suspended on the icy updraught. Then the flag fell to the ground and the blunderbuss discharged.

The race had begun!

Drakon leapt ahead with the others, his sudden burst of forward momentum spinning the wheels wildly, and Anna felt the carriage skidding sickeningly across the black ice. Theirs was not the only carriage that was out of control. All across the river the drivers tried to keep on course as the horses flailed about in a mad panic. Their footing failed them and the horses tripped and stumbled trying to gain purchase upon the glassy surface.

Anna used the reins to steady Drakon, and braced her feet against the rew bargeboard so that she would not be flung from the carriage as they lurched, tilting over to one side. And then Drakon's grip on the ice became sure and strong. His powerful knees locked and he regained control of the carriage behind him. The grey stallion was facing straight down the river, moving like an arrow, accelerating with such speed that within a few strides he was a full carriage-length in front of the other horses. Anna left the commotion of the other drivers behind her in the wind and for a moment all she could hear was the furious *tchok-tchok* of Drakon's enormous hooves striking the ice, cutting like blades into the frozen surface of the river.

But Anna was not alone as she pulled free of the pack. To the left, she caught a glimpse of the dark bay Kabarda moving up the ice strongly on the outside track. The Kabarda's choppy, fervent gait pitched him swiftly across the ice. His strides were even quicker than Drakon's and Count Smirnov drove his horse on, lashing him again and again with the whip.

Anna took a sideways glance at the Count. He was manoeuvring his stallion over the ice to get closer to hers. On the slick surface of the frozen Voronezh all it would take was a shoulder charge from the Kabarda stallion and Anna and her carriage would be sent spiralling into a crash!

"Drakon!" Anna's voice cried out above the howl of the wind. "Drakon, we need to go. Now!"

At the sound of her voice, it was as if Drakon found his wings. His strides stretched out and devoured the ice beneath him. Surefooted and bold, he struck out a rhythm with his enormous hooves that seemed to suction to the ice.

The Kabarda's strides were quick but they lacked the length and grace of Drakon's. The grey stallion was pulling away from the dark bay horse, moving further and further ahead. The Kabarda was already spent from his initial frantic burst of speed. His pace began to falter and he had nothing left in reserve. Compared to Drakon, it was as if he had come to a standstill. For the Kabarda, the race was over.

Anna kept casting backward glances over her shoulder, wondering where the next challenge might come from. The other carriages were so far behind they were no more than misty black shapes falling away in the blur of the swirling snow.

Up ahead the forest loomed closer, the snow-frosted treetops tinted rose-gold in the glow of the morning light, casting long shadows all the way to the black ice of the river. Anna turned the carriage now, heading towards the firs, and drove Drakon on. She kept the pace, asking him to stride out as fast as they could race towards the shoreline.

As the wheels struck land, Anna was jolted about as the smoothness of the ice was replaced by ruts and hollows. The carriage keeled left and right beneath her, being shaken like a toy rattle in the hand of a giant. When they hit a deep rut Anna was thrown with a thump out of her seat, biting her tongue and tasting blood as she crashed hard on to the bench seat.

She slowed Drakon's trot so that she could keep the carriage under control, but even at half the speed they had been doing on the ice the going was so bumpy! Every single bounce reverberated painfully through her body, making it hard to keep hold of the reins. At times the carriage would lurch out from underneath her and she would find herself struggling just to stay on board.

The shadows of the fir trees closed in as they carved a path through the gloom into the heart of the forest. Anna chose her route carefully. Some of the tracks were broader than others. Some became narrower or tapered into dead ends. She had to remember the right one or all the time they had gained on the ice could easily be lost again.

Anna cast a glance up at the treetops and caught a glimpse of sky flickering past. Vasily had been right; ominous snow clouds had gathered, making the heavens above so dark it was as if night had fallen.

In this gloomy half-light, filtered through tall trees, shadows fell across Drakon's grey dapples. Anna looked ahead, sighting her route. The excitement of the black ice was behind them and the rhythm of the race had changed. This would be a long journey into the taiga. They had many more hours to go and Drakon's hooves settled into a hypnotic *tchok-tchok* that soon became one with Anna's heartbeat as they drove on into the dark woods.

***

All this time the carriage axle had held strong. Black oak is a sturdy wood, almost as hard as pig iron, and the construction of the axle stood fast despite Ivan's sabotage attempts. On the frozen river it had given very little, the carriage wheels skating evenly across the surface. On land, however, the bumps and dips of the potholes jarred the frame with every stride, doing exactly what Ivan had anticipated. With each jolt the axle wood was weakening, the splits deepening, the carriage beginning to sag.

Anna did not realise any of this. As she drove Drakon on, her only thoughts were to make it to the Bridge of the Single Pine, fasten her colours and then turn again for home.

When she saw a boulder peeping up out of the snow in the track ahead she tried to avoid it, swinging right, but amongst the trees she couldn't risk veering too far off course. She thought nothing about letting the left-hand front wheel clip the rock as she drove past.

Suddenly there was a crack like a blunderbuss, a noise that echoed through the snowy hush of the woods. Then Anna felt the world give way underneath her.

She screamed as the front wheels tilted and then collapsed entirely, caving in and plummeting the chassis of the carriage downwards, ploughing the bench seat hard into the snow. Anna was jettisoned as if she were a stone launched from a catapult. She saw the flash of Drakon's gigantic hooves come over the top of her and she remembered thinking how odd it was to see the undersides of his feet and how very big they were so close to her face. Then she felt a metal horseshoe strike hard at her temple and she hit the snowy ground face-first. The whiteness all around her became black and Anna was gone.

***

It was the snow that roused her. The icy cold on her skin prickled her awake, making her cough and sputter. All around her was a scene of devastation. The carriage was a wreck, the wooden bench seat in pieces, the wheels tilted inwards sickeningly, the spokes splintered and broken.

"Drakon?" Anna's voice was shaky. "Drakon!"

When the carriage had collapsed it brought her horse down with it. The sudden impact had dropped the grey stallion to his knees and now the harnesses held him there, pinned to the ground unable to move.

Drakon had dug himself through the snow to the hard dirt below, and streaks of mud and crimson blood stained the white drifts all around him. He must have been struggling the whole time that Anna had been unconscious. The wooden strut on the left side of the harnesses had snapped in two and Drakon had been impaled on the wooden shaft. Blood was seeping into the snow as he lay there, a froth of sweat on his neck and his flanks wet and heaving with exhaustion.

Anna rose trembling to her hands and knees, her

head swimming as she took deep, panicky breaths. She got up and began to stagger through the snow towards her horse. As she moved closer, Drakon began thrashing and flinging himself against the harnesses.

"*Niet! Niet!*" Anna commanded. " Drakon, please! You are making it worse!"

Blood was staining Drakon's grey dapples as it trickled down to the snow beneath him.

Never before had the stallion looked quite so dragon-like as he did now, surrounded by the wreckage of the carriage and the blood-stained snow, plumes of steam shooting from his nostrils and his eyes wild with fear. Drakon flung himself against the harness, lashing out with his hooves, trying to work his way free. Anna threw herself down at his side in the snow, ripping off her gloves so that her half-frozen fingers could work loose the harness straps. Drakon was in danger of hurting them both with his wild lunges. Anna kept a watchful eye on his flailing front legs, anxious to avoid being struck down.

"Wait! Drakon! Let me finish… ugh…" She

struggled to undo the straps, her hands working feverishly. But when she had loosened the buckles Drakon made matters worse by thrashing about, tightening them again.

"Stop it! Please!" At last she managed to keep him steady long enough and she felt the final buckle release. He was free!

Anna flung herself clear of the stallion as Drakon, desperate to escape, lunged up with a grunt, falling forward on to his knees and then rising up on legs still shaking with the shock of his ordeal.

Now that he was upright the gouge in his shoulder looked worse than ever, but miraculously he was not lame. And as Anna examined the shattered remains of the carriage, she could scarcely believe they had got off so lightly. Somehow she and her horse had survived a terrible crash. Now Anna had to save them from the wilderness itself.

Her mind racing with adrenalin, she began undoing the straps of the harness from the struts, fashioning them into a set of reins. She attached these to Drakon's bridle so that she would have something to lead him by, and then after pulling on her gloves, slowly, gingerly, she clucked the big grey horse forward, away from a scene of the devastation that could have killed them both.

The hooded crows who had been hopping about, waiting and hoping in vain that there might be a meal for them, pecked at the bloodied snow and searched the carriage remains. Then they flew back up to their vantage point in the tops of the trees. Anna looked up at the scavengers circling and imagined how the wreckage must appear from above, a dark carcass with its broken bones laid bare against the stark white snow. And leading away from it, two sets of tracks, footprints side by side. The marks of Anna and her horse as they walked away.

The snow was falling heavily, and in the distance came a mournful howl. It was the cry of the wilderness, of the taiga.

The call of the timber wolf.

CHAPTER 13

Winter's Howl

The wolf's howl was a lonely bay that filled the woods with its haunting echo. The sound made the hairs rise on the back of Anna's neck, putting fire in her blood, making her pulse quicken.

"Come on, Drakon! We need to get moving!"

There was a slim chance that one of the other carriage racers might come across their wreckage and follow her, but Anna knew it was unlikely. Before the crash she had taken backwoods paths and now she had veered off completely, to seek the shortest route home. With dusk approaching, Anna's only goal was to get to the estate, following her inner compass, going south. Through the falling snow she could still make out the mountains to the east, the deep forest glades to the west, and she knew she was heading in the right direction.

Although they were taking the shortest route as the crow flies, it was not easy terrain. The ground beneath the snow was pocked with massive potholes beneath the smooth white surface. At times the drifts were so deep Anna would find herself up to her waist as if she were wading a river. All the same, she refused to mount Drakon. She worried that his shoulder wound could not withstand the weight of a rider on his back. And so she walked alongside him, feeling the snow soaking her clothes and turning them stiff with ice, her feet becoming numb and leaden.

In her wake, Anna left black holes where her feet had plunged into the snow as she struggled onward. Drakon, however, left something more. Red drops of blood, like berries on the white snow. A scent trail. In the far distance, a timber wolf had picked up the smell. His lone cry became a howl of hunger and excitement. Soon he was joined by a wild chorus as the rest of the pack picked up the scent. The wolves united in the hunt. They were coming for Anna and Drakon.

The five black shapes first appeared as specks in the distance, but all too soon Anna could see them looming closer. She was reminded of that very morning on the ice when the dark shapes of the carriages behind them had spurred her on. At the time it had felt so vital to stay ahead of them, to keep the lead. As if her life had depended on keeping out of reach of her rivals. How ridiculous! What a fool she had been to care about something so completely trivial. Alone in the vastness of the taiga with the wolf cries and the night closing in fast, Anna understood that the only thing that mattered now was survival.

"Hurry, Drakon!" Anna began to drag her horse by the reins, imploring him to move faster. But even as she did this she knew in her heart that there was no way to outrun the wolves. The pack were built for speed in the snow and with Drakon injured, they could never keep ahead of the timber wolves all the way back to Khrenovsky.

Out here in open terrain the wolves would run them down easily. Her only chance was to get Drakon to the woods. There they could stand their ground and try to fight rather than run and die. In the grove of trees ahead, in amongst the firs, Anna might be able to find some weapon, a stout bough, something she could use.

"We need to reach the trees, Drakon." She grabbed at the harnesses. "I'm sorry to do this but we will never make it if I am on foot…"

The weight of Anna's snow-soaked skirts made it even harder to pull herself up on to Drakon's back. She kept sliding down, frustrated and panicked as her efforts brought them to a standstill. Her blood was pounding as she leapt up again and again and the wolf howls grew louder in her ears. Finally, using every last scrap of strength that she possessed, she kicked off the ground with all her might and managed to fling a leg over Drakon's back and cling on to right herself. She snatched hold of the harnesses and gave her stallion a swift kick to urge him on. She had never kicked her horse before but Drakon responded exactly as she had hoped he would, with a snort of shock and then a great leap forward.

The horse moved straight into a gallop, and Anna clung to his mane as he leapt through the snowdrifts like a gazelle, flinging his forelegs high into the air to rise above the drifts and then sinking again with every stride. He used his powerful hindquarters, rearing to get momentum and then crashing down, ploughing onward like a ship through rough seas.

The immense effort to gallop like this through the snow with the girl on his back was exhausting him, but Anna drove the horse on, staying with him stride for stride. "Go, Drakon! Run!"

Anna cast a fearful glance behind her and saw that the timber wolves were even closer. They were no longer abstract black shapes in the distance, but real creatures, snarling and salivating, bounding inexorably onwards with the smell of Drakon's blood filling their nostrils, their jaws open wide in anticipation.

"Go, Drakon!" Anna urged her horse to even greater speed through the snowdrifts, ploughing his way towards the trees ahead.

The firs were dense, and when they finally reached the woods Anna was almost knocked off her horse as they pushed their way through the low branches laden with snow. There was no path, so she had to force her way through a tangle of tree boughs, using one arm to hold on to her horse and the other to protect her face from the firs. Suddenly the trees around them disappeared completely. They had reached a natural clearing within the forest. Here, the snow had barely penetrated and the ground was lightly dusted with white flakes on the dense brown floor of pine needles.

Anna flung herself down from Drakon's back and clawed about in the snow, searching for a large branch. She picked up a stick the size of her arm and then discarded it in a panic. Too short and not sturdy enough! She needed something bigger.

The howls were getting louder, closer. Picking up the same stick that she had thrown away just a moment before, she raced back to Drakon's side.

The grey stallion was quivering with fear, his flanks heaving, every muscle twitching. The wolf cries had awoken in him that natural urge that lies in all horses: the instinct to take flight.

Run, Drakon's blood was telling him. *Run.*

Blood is powerful. But it is not destiny.

Drakon's ears flattened hard against his head in fury. He trembled beside Anna but he did not leave her. He could have run, but instead he stood there, loyal and steadfast.

And then the baying stopped. An eerie stillness filled the clearing. Anna caught a glimpse of grey fur between the pines. The wolves were there, hidden by the trees. They stalked their prey, paws padding silently across the snow, creeping ever closer. Anna held up the bough, preparing herself for battle.

"Do you see them?" Anna asked the horse. "Drakon…"

Suddenly, in a frenzy of snarling, the wolves crashed into the clearing.

There were five of them, but three were barely more than cubs. The younger wolves were all pale grey like their mother, but the adult male wolf had a thick black coat that faded to charcoal at the tips.

Crab-walking back and forth with shoulders hunched and mouth open to show his dripping fangs, the male wolf took charge of the scene. As he snarled and snapped at the female and the cubs to keep them in line, Anna thought of the timber wolves in their cage at Khrenovsky. When meat was thrown in at dinnertime the pack leader always grabbed his share first and ate greedily before his cubs. In the same way, these wild wolf cubs hung back and waited. Anna knew they would not attack unless the black wolf gave the order.

He padded back and forth, edging forward on silent paws until he was so close to Anna she could smell his fetid, hot breath, and see the gleam of saliva on his fangs.

Shaking, she tightened her grip on the bough, readying herself to swing it.

The black wolf gave a bloodcurdling growl and came at Anna in a blind rush of slavering jaws and cold, white fangs. He leapt with such ferocious speed that she had no time to raise the weapon. Anna felt the blow of the body crashing against her, knocking her to the frozen ground. But it was not the wolf that had struck her.

It was Drakon.

The grey stallion had pushed her aside to face

the wolf himself. Anna had no idea how Drakon had moved so quickly. One moment the wolf was leaping for her throat and the next Drakon had plunged between the predator and his mistress. Blocking the wolf's path, Drakon went up on his hindquarters and struck with his front hooves. He caught the wolf a vicious blow that sent the creature reeling. Dazed, the wolf rose to his feet to find Drakon towering above him, trembling with fury, his ears flattened against his head, hooves pawing the ground.

The timber wolf gave a low growl, and prepared himself to attack again. This time he would not do so alone. Already the other wolves were circling, ready to lunge and strike at the grey stallion. They would use their superior numbers to take him by surprise while the black wolf attacked from the front. Drakon tensed his muscles, bracing himself for the impact.

The huge black timber wolf took a stride and then threw himself forward, leaping through the air, ready to strike Drakon with the full force of his weight. They were like mountains about to collide.

In all this time, none of them had noticed a shadow creeping quietly between the trees. Not Anna or Drakon or the wolf pack. A master of camouflage, the shadow was obscured in the half-light of dusk. His markings kept him well hidden while the soft pads of his giant paws made no noise on the carpet of fallen pine needles and snow.

In the gloom of the woods, he had watched as the wolves gathered, cornering Anna and Drakon. And as the black wolf flung himself through the air to close his deadly jaws round Drakon's throat, the shadow knew his moment had come.

With a devastating roar that shook the air like a mountain avalanche, the tiger struck the black timber wolf with all his might, toppling him off balance, bringing both of them crashing down to the ground.

The wolf barely had a chance to lift his head. With one glorious sweep of his enormous paw, the tiger hurled him into a tree trunk on the far side of the clearing. This time the wolf did not rebound. He lay there yelping pitifully; a cry of pain and defeat.

With his tail slung low, the vanquished black timber wolf abandoned his pack and ran off into the trees. The four remaining wolves circled the tiger, posturing and snarling, shoulders rolling as they ducked and nipped at him, manoeuvring like boxers looking to land a blow.

The tiger let them dance and weave, with an air of calm disdain. Then, as though tired of this game, he struck back with a brutal finality. Taking on all four wolves at once, he threw them about as if they were no more than playthings. When the tiger had finished, the snow was streaked with blood, and the timber wolves were scattering, tails between legs, limping away with their bellies empty.

The tiger watched them go and then turned to Anna and Drakon.

He moved with the fluid grace of a dancer, paws crossing step by step, his amber gaze fixed on Anna and a strange deep growl coming from his throat. Only one who knows tigers intimately would have understood it, for it was a sound not often heard in nature. It was a tiger's purr.

"Boris?"

Anna could scarcely believe it.

"Boris? *Borenka?* Is it you? Is it really you?"

And then she was running to him through the snow, and the big cat was roaring his strange melodic growl-purr and she had her arms round his neck and she was crushing the tiger to her chest, holding him as tight as she could.

"Borenka!" Anna buried her face in his orange-and-black striped coat. "I never thought I would see you again. Oh, but you have grown! Look how enormous you are!"

She held him close for the longest time, feeling the opulence of his plush coat, so soft and delicious just as it had been when he was only a cub. She buried her head again and again in his wonderful fur and then, when at last she let him go, Boris padded across the snow towards Drakon.

The horse and the tiger stood facing each other, battle-scarred and exhausted. And then, with a gentle nicker, the horse did what he had always done. He reached down his dragon-face and, opening his nostrils wide, he inhaled the tiger's breath. Muzzle to muzzle, horse and tiger, bonded by their love for Anna and their love for each other.

***

In the hours that followed, Boris and Drakon were like old comrades, walking side by side in companionable silence. It was only when they drew close to the borders of the Khrenovsky estate that Anna noticed the tiger slowing his stride. He was falling back, distancing himself from the girl and the horse.

As the snow fell harder, she began to lose sight of Boris. And then she turned to look for him and realised that he was gone.

Anna did not call his name, even though she knew he would have come if she had done so. It had to be this way. They were too close to the estate – it was not safe for the tiger to be here.

And so they walked on, just Anna and Drakon. The snowdrifts were waist-deep and it was a desperate struggle to walk. She could not bring herself to remount Drakon. It seemed unfair to ask her wounded horse to carry her when he was every bit as exhausted as she was. They ploughed on side by side, too tired to do anything more than trudge onwards, putting one foot doggedly in front of the next.

When Anna saw the twinkling of the palace lights on the horizon, she knew she was heading in the right direction. Then the blizzard set in, just as Vasily said it would. As the snowstorm raged around them, the lights on the horizon were completely obscured. Anna and Drakon were alone in the dark.

"Come on! It is not much further," Anna insisted. "We must keep moving, Drakon…"

Suddenly, the grey stallion lurched sideways, his legs buckling beneath him.

"Drakon!"

Anna flung herself at him, fingers twisting into the rope of his mane, trying in vain to pull him to his feet. "Drakon, please! Please…"

The snow stung her face as he went down.

"*Niet!*" She tore out chunks of mane as she tried to drag him to his feet. "*Niet!* Drakon! Get up!"

Removing her fur coat with trembling hands, she

laid it on top of the horse and burrowed underneath, warming both of them as best she could.

"It's just like the old days, Drakon… riding in the woods…" Anna murmured as she nestled into the crook of her horse's forelimbs, tucked up against his chest.

"Remember how we slept underneath the stars? With the rugs laid beneath us and Vasily tending the fire pit to heat his urn of spiced honey tea and Igor whimpering as he dreamt of chasing timber wolves…"

Darling Igor! Her father would never understand that her borzoi was the best hound he had ever bred. He would have ended Igor's precious bloodline without a second thought, given the chance.

"He would have killed you too, Drakon," she whispered. "Long ago, if I had given him the chance. But I gave you life and I have loved you with all of my heart. You are everything to me, Drakon."

Anna could hear the horse breathing, feel the faint rise and fall of his exhausted ribcage.

Trying to warm herself a little, she pulled the fur coat up to her chest. As she did so her gloved fingertips brushed against the filigree chain round her neck.

With trembling hands she clasped the priceless diamond and raised it up to her face so that she could gaze upon its dark beauty.

Summoning all her remaining strength, she stared hard into the stone. The brilliant-cut jewel refracted and reflected the light, splintering the world into a million tiny pieces as infinite as the snowflakes that swirled around her.

Visions cut like shards of glass into her consciousness. She saw the amber glint of a tiger's eye, the flash of his stripes and the low rumble of his growl. And then she saw the girl with the pink horse. Her stallion was beautiful like Drakon, dancing and stepping in time to music. There were lights shining like stars above her...

Anna's hands clutched at her throat and then the diamond teardrop slipped from her fingers as she fell back against Drakon, her body cold and limp, lost to the frozen Russian night.

Chapter 14

Reach for the Stars

"Into the piaffe now! And there you go!" George Mueller slapped his hands down on his thighs. "That one was perfect. A ten, Valentina, a ten! You and Sasha can finish up now."

The girl mounted on the pink stallion allowed herself just the hint of a smile as she slipped the reins and let Sasha walk out, cooling him down.

Over the past six months, Valentina had found herself in awe of the ability of the Russian Federation's head coach to always push her that bit harder, making her step up her game until she was riding better than she ever thought possible. "We are perfectionists, you and I," the head coach would tell her. "You, Valentina, never settle for anything less than a ten."

And perfection was what she would need to impress the judges on the international circuit. Them and everyone else, it seemed. Olga had gone into meltdown last week when George Mueller announced that Valentina and Sasha had made the team for the international competition. "It is an embarrassment to Russia! We will be known as the circus freaks!"

With the Stockholm World Games only days away, Valentina's greatest concern was that the judges would look down their noses at Sasha and refuse to give top marks to such a strange-looking horse with no proper breeding.

"Really though, how could anyone not think you are beautiful?" Valentina murmured to Sasha as she did up his stable rug. The pink stallion responded with a gentle nicker and then he burrowed his enormous head into Valentina's chest once more and gazed up at her. Valentina marvelled at his long, dark, thick eyelashes and his almond-shaped eyes like those of a cat, the taper of his muzzle, the way the nostrils flared, and his massive powerful jaw. Sasha's profile was so incredible. Oscar had once said to Valentina that her horse reminded him of a dragon. A beautiful, pink dragon.

Valentina was so proud to be riding in the Federation colours. When the announcement had been made about who was on the team, George Mueller had presented Valentina with a set of "tails": the elegant riding jacket that she would wear for the Grand Prix. Then Molly and Oscar had surprised her with their own gift.

"I know everyone is wearing helmets these days," Molly said. "But we thought since you used to be a circus girl that a top hat was more appropriate."

Valentina had almost cried when she opened the package. Inside was a perfect black silk topper, the sort that professional dressage riders wore. The sort that Valentina would now wear.

***

A dressage "test", even at Grand Prix level, is no more than a series of movements: distinct manoeuvres

235

such as half-passes and flying changes, extended trots and collected canters, which are marked by the judges with a score from one to ten. These scores, along with bonus points for precision, paces, and the stylishness and expertise of the rider, add up to a final tally. At times the marks are so close that the tiniest percentage point can make the difference between winning and losing.

This was not the case for Valentina Romanov in Stockholm. As the numbers flashed up in brilliant neon above the grandstand, there was a dumbstruck silence from the crowd. The Russian rider had just scored an appalling 55.4 per cent for her first test.

Until Valentina saw the results in glaring neon she had hoped against hope that she was simply being too critical of herself. In her heart though she knew their half-passes had been weak, the canter off-beat, and the trot had lacked connection. When the score went up on the board Valentina was not surprised. She was merely devastated.

"It is my fault!" she told George Mueller as she threw herself down from Sasha's back and began to untack the pink stallion. "You should never have brought me here. I have let the whole team down!"

"Do not talk like that," George Mueller said firmly. "I am not interested in melodrama or blame. We need to find out what went wrong here today. Valentina, you rode like a beginner. No strength to your legs, no timing. Your hands were shaking. What happened to you?"

"Nothing! That is me! I am a terrible rider! Did you see my pirouettes?" Valentina was in tears. "They were awful! I got a 4.5!"

"Valentina. Stop torturing yourself! The point is we must learn from this experience and look to the next one. Always riding forward, Valentina. Now, tell me, honestly. Why did you lose your focus? What happened?"

Valentina could not look at him. "You're going to think this is stupid... I got stage fright."

George Mueller looked stunned. "But you have spent your whole life under the bright lights, Valentina. You are a performer! It is what you do!"

"Yes, but not in front of *these* people!" Valentina said. "I know how they judge me and my horse. I know what they say. They are all just like Olga –

saying how unsuitable Sasha is for the sport, a pink beast with no bloodline. That he will never have the paces of a Warmblood. That he is ugly and I am nothing more than a jumped-up circus kid. And then you tell me to hold my head up and ride elegantly into the arena and impress everyone? How can I do this? How can I magically perform as if I am the greatest in the world when I know what they really think? It is impossible!"

"Look at me, Valentina," George Mueller said. "Please, look at me."

Valentina raised her face. She could see that George Mueller had tears in his eyes.

"I forget, Valentina, just how far you have come and how fast. I prepared you as a rider to win, but I did not prepare you personally for the rigours of competitive life."

The head coach put his arm round her. "Valentina, sadly I cannot tell you that you are wrong. There will always be those who whisper behind their hands and laugh at you from the grandstands. But is it really those people that you are striving to impress? They have made their minds up about you and your pink circus horse, and their minds are terrible, closed vessels. They are not what we ride for, Valentina. We ride only for the truth and purity and beauty of this sport. I have seen in you, Valentina, such great ability. You could be the very best in the world. A perfect ten. As for Sasha, I would not trade him for any horse in the world!"

This got a smile from Valentina.

"There! That is the Valentina that I want to see!" George Mueller smiled back. "The girl with spirit, with fire in her blood. Do not take this setback and go home a loser, Valentina. Use it to make you stronger. Anyone can be great in victory. But a true hero, they will be even greater in moments of defeat. It is at the times when we are at our worst that we have the clearest vision of what we need to become."

George Mueller walked over to Sasha and slipped the saddle off the pink stallion's back.

"And Valentina, although Sasha possesses no papers to prove it, I can tell you exactly what breed he is. His regal bearing, his conformation and most of all his loyal and unwavering courage tell me. He is an Orlov Trotter, the most noble and ancient breed in all of Russia. Never before has an Orlov represented Russia, or been ridden in the Grand Prix, but your Sasha is undoubtedly of this lineage. He is brilliant, Valentina, I have complete faith that he will prove himself. And when you believe that too, then you and Sasha will be the greatest dressage combination the world has ever seen."

That night, when the other riders were all asleep in their bunk beds, Valentina sat up at the table and took out her diary. She made a note of all the dates: the competitions, the training sessions to come and the final countdown to the twenty-third of July. On that date, she drew five interlinking circles.

A secret code, an unbelievable dream. A reminder of her goal.

The symbol of the Olympic Games.

Chapter 15

Frozen

"Igor? Igor? What is it? What have you found?"
The voice was so faint, it was like someone
calling from far away, and yet Anna knew that they
were right beside her. She wanted to cry out, but it
was as if her voice had left her body far behind. She
was sinking down, down into the snow never to rise
up again. She was falling under the black surface of
the river and the light was fading. Anna was lost.

And then, like a diver breaking the surface, she
gasped air again. She was freezing cold but she was
alive. And there was something hot and searing
against her icy cheek. It was the pink, moist tongue
of a hound.

"Igor…?" Anna murmured.

"Anna!"

Vasily fell to his knees in the snow, and threw his arms round her.

"Anna! Anna!"

Anna opened her eyes.

"You're alive!"

Anna smiled at him. "You told me to come home safe," she said softly. "Here I am."

***

Later, Vasily told Anna all that had happened while she was missing. "All the drivers had returned by dusk except for you. It seemed very strange that once you had gone beyond the woods none of them saw you or Drakon again. Your father ordered a mass search across the taiga. He sent men out beyond the gates of the estate to hunt in every direction. Then a rider returned saying he had found the debris of your carriage but no sign of you or Drakon. Your father sent fresh horses to the scene immediately. I rode with Igor at my side, but as Count Orlov and his men headed out of the gates of the estate towards the barren taiga, your wolfhound suddenly put up a hunting cry and bolted in the opposite direction. Igor raced back across the estate, heading for the woods by the palace. I tried calling him to heel, but he wouldn't listen to me. He must have picked up your scent on the night air."

Anna was surprised. "Borzoi are bred to hunt by sight, not scent."

"I know." Vasily shook his head. "And yet he found your trail better than any bloodhound. He bolted so swiftly I had to press my horse to a gallop to keep up with him."

"So he led you to me?"

"Not quite. When he reached the dark woods I lost sight of him. I could hear his baying and I knew he was close but, I could not locate him. The blizzard had closed in and I was searching blindly when I saw something glow. It looked like a star, it shimmered so brightly. Then I heard Igor resume his baying call – it was coming from the same place as the light. So I ran towards it and that was when I found you."

"What was it?" Anna asked him. "This light that

you saw shining? For I had no fire, no torch with me."

Vasily gestured to the black teardrop glittering at her throat. "It was your diamond, Lady Anna. The light was coming from your necklace. I cannot explain it, but that is what led me to you."

***

At first, Anna had been too afraid to ask Vasily about Drakon. Her thoughts went back to that fateful expedition on the frozen river, the day she lost Smetanka. After the race across the taiga, Drakon had been in a terrible state, worse than she was. She remembered the way her brave stallion had fallen, the coldness of his body in the snowdrifts. She felt the tears welling in her eyes. "Vasily? My horse…"

"No, no, do not cry, Lady Anna," Vasily reassured her. "He is alive! As soon as you are strong enough, I will take you to the stables to see him."

"I want to go now," Anna insisted.

Vasily shook his head. "In your state? Katia would be furious with me."

Anna sat up in her bed, her head swimming, her skin drained even paler than usual, and looked Vasily square in the eyes. "And if you do not take me now I will be furious."

Vasily carried her to the stables in his arms. Anna was too weak to walk, but she could still talk and they spent the entire time discussing the race. She was pleased to hear that the Kabarda stallion had lost in a surprise victory for Count Petrov and his skinny ewe-necked chestnut.

"Count Smirnov is demanding a rematch," Vasily told Anna. "There is a grand dinner tonight and the Empress is going to award the winner a golden sash…"

"Sasha and I were in the lead, you know," she told Vasily quietly. "Way out in front of the rest. If the axle hadn't broken…"

Vasily glanced at her warily.

"What is it?" she demanded.

"I am not sure," the groom replied carefully. "Only, I checked the carriage just a week before the race and its axle was solid. I cannot imagine how it could have broken… unless it was sabotaged."

"You think someone did this to me on purpose?" Anna could not believe what she was hearing.

Vasily looked anxious. "Lady Anna, you must tell no one about any of this. To accuse one of your competitors of such a crime would be dangerous."

"You are right." Anna nodded but her brain was whirring.

They walked on to the stables in contemplative silence as Anna tried to think back to those moments before the race began. She had seen Smirnov and Petrov lining up to race against her, but neither of them had shown any twitch or tell, no giveaway sign of what they might have been plotting. Then she thought of her brother Ivan, standing on the palace steps beside the Empress with his goblet held aloft, mouthing to her: *Good luck, Sister.*

"Drakon is in the first stall on the left," Vasily told Anna, lowering her to the ground so that she could walk the last few steps on her own.

The grey stallion was staring at the wall in the furthest corner of his stall. Anna unbolted the door of the loose box and walked inside.

"Drakon?"

At the sound of Anna's voice the horse raised his head. His ears swivelled backwards, but he did not turn. It was as if he refused to believe what he was hearing.

"Drakon," she said again, softly this time, "it's me."

With a snort of consternation, Drakon spun on his hocks and faced her. He stood there in the darkness, his enormous dragon's head with its wide flared nostrils as beautiful as she had ever seen it.

Then the stallion's whole demeanour was suddenly transformed. He began vigorously shaking his head, swinging his whole neck up and down, his eyes bright and shining as he trotted up to Anna, nickering and snorting. He plunged his muzzle into the crook of her armpit as if demanding that she throw her arms round him, which of course she did.

"I thought you were dead, Drakon, I thought we both were…" Anna felt the tears welling in her eyes. She held her horse close, and whispered in his ear. "You are truly the greatest horse in all of Russia. No one could ever doubt it."

***

Katia did not approve of Anna going to the stables, and she was even less enthusiastic about the idea of her attending the grand dinner planned for that evening. "You are still exhausted, Lady Anna," the head housekeeper insisted. "You should be in bed!"

"And then when I am well again all the guests will be gone and Khrenovsky will be empty as it always is," Anna argued. "Please, Katia! If I feel unwell I will return to my room, I promise. I so want to hear the guests gossiping and see Count Smirnov trying to be gracious when really he is furious that Count Petrov has beaten him..."

"Very well then." Katia took the gown that she had put in the wardrobe back out again and laid it on the bed. "I suppose a hearty feast will do you some good – there is venison I hear, cooked with snowberries and violets. But I shall be keeping an eye on you and if you begin to grow paler than you already are, you will be heading upstairs."

"Yes, Katia!" Anna was delighted.

She put on the pale pink chiffon gown and sat down in front of the dressing table. Igor sat with her as she did her make-up.

"Do you hear that, Igor?" Anna stroked the borzoi. "There is venison for me to smuggle back to you."

Igor placed his head in her lap appreciatively and looked up at her with his dark eyes shining. Ever since he had found her in the snow he had not left her side.

At the door of her bedroom she was about to tell him to stay but she was unable to resist those dark, soulful eyes.

"You can accompany me as far as the door of the grand dining room," she told Igor. "But no further than that, *milochka*."

They walked together through the stately hallway, Anna's heels and Igor's claws click-clacking against the cool, marble floors. As she prepared to descend the staircase that led to the grand dining room, Igor began to give a low, fretful growl. Anna looked up and saw Ivan waiting for her at the foot of the stairs.

"Sister!" he greeted her, with a suspicious degree of warmth. "I have come to accompany you to the dinner."

Anna glared at him as he walked up the stairs and took Anna's right hand in his own, bending low to give it a kiss.

Beside her, Igor bared his teeth, the hackles rising on his back, his growl deepening.

"Such a loyal hound," Ivan sneered. "They say he was the one who saved your life yesterday."

Anna's heart was pounding, although she was not sure why. "He led Vasily to me," she agreed. "I would have died without them. And Boris of course."

"Yes, of course." Ivan's face was dark. "The wolves would have got you for certain when that axle snapped if it were not for your precious tiger. Your little team of protectors, always sticking up for you."

He put his arm out for Anna to take to descend the stairs, but she recoiled.

"How do you know about the axle?"

Standing at Anna's side, Igor began to growl more fiercely. Ivan looked down at the borzoi and grimaced. "Your bodyguard is always here, isn't he?" Ivan glowered at the hound. "Well, you will need him, little sister," his tone was sinister. "For I am always here too. And accidents can keep happening without warning…"

As Ivan said these words, Anna suddenly became

aware of how empty the palace hallways were and how high and steep the marble staircase was. As Ivan reached for her arm again she pulled away from him. He stepped forward to grab at her, but the borzoi was too quick for him.

In a flash, Igor leapt, and before Ivan could dodge to the side the wolfhound had Anna's brother sprawled on his back on the marble floor. Snarling protectively, Igor sat on Ivan's chest, holding him down.

"Get your beast off me!" Ivan ordered. "Make him stand down!"

Anna looked hard at her brother and then simply said, "Igor, stay."

Then she skipped down the marble stairs and hurried to the grand dining hall.

At its entrance, the doorman in the golden costume insisted on announcing her to the room in the formal fashion:

"Lady Anna of Khrenovsky!" To Anna's great surprise, the entire dining room rose from their tables and rose to their feet to clink their glasses with their forks and applaud.

"What is all this about?" Anna wondered. "Why do they cheer for me?"

Then Count Smirnov took it upon himself to stride across the room and greet her warmly, bowing and grinning as if she were his long-lost best friend.

"How perfect that you should arrive at this moment, Lady Anna." He gestured towards the table. "We have just been talking about you. Or I should say we were talking about your horse. I have just agreed terms with your father to bring my mares to Khrenovsky in the spring. They shall be put into foal by the magnificent stallion, Drakon!"

Count Petrov had also sprung up to her side. "Do not think you can jump the queue, Smirnov," he scolded. "The greatest horse in all of Russia will serve my mares first. I shall have many Orlov Trotters in my stables before long!"

For despite Anna and Drakon's failure to win the race, the brilliance of Drakon was celebrated by all who had seen his display on the black ice of the Voronezh river. This strangely conformed horse had led out at such speed that he left all other competitors in his wake, crossing the taiga with an exhibition of stamina that certainly would have won the race had misfortune not intervened. And then there was the loyalty of a horse who would protect his mistress by risking his own life against a pack of timber wolves, fighting valiantly side by side with a Siberian tiger!

"Lady Anna?" It was the Empress's chief aide. He leant past Smirnov and Petrov to take her by the hand with a gracious bow. "Her Majesty requests that you accompany me to join her. You will be the guest at her right hand this evening."

Anna looked across the room to see the Empress sitting at the head of the table. She was wearing a teal and peacock-blue gown, trimmed with lace round the neckline, her hair powdered in a vibrant shade of lilac.

"Are you sure?" Anna could not believe it. "She has requested *me*?"

"Yes, my lady," the aide replied. "Her Majesty desires your presence immediately; dinner is about to begin."

Anna felt certain as she walked through the dining room that she was going to stumble or fall and make a fool of herself somehow.

When she sat down next to Empress Catherine, her hands were shaking so badly she hoped dinner would never come because she could not pick up her cutlery.

"Are you nervous, dear one?" Empress Catherine placed her own hand on top of Anna's and gave it a comforting squeeze. "It is such a delight to have you to myself tonight. We shall talk about a great many things…" The Empress smiled. "But first let me attend to the formalities."

Tapping her raised glass with her fork, the Empress engaged the room and all the assorted company rose to their feet. "Ladies and gentlemen, it is wonderful to enjoy such a feast with you on this cold winter night. I am sure you will join me in offering congratulations to Count Petrov, whose chestnut stallion was the winner of yesterday's race across the taiga."

The Empress paused. "And to Count Orlov. Truly he has proven himself to be breeder of the finest horses in all of Russia! And he has provided us with this marvellous feast, so… *Bon appétit!*"

Count Orlov, sitting to the left of the Empress, looked delighted with this acknowledgement. As Her Majesty took her chair once more, she leant across to him and said loud enough for Anna to hear, "You have always boasted of the bloodlines at the Khrenovsky estate, Count Orlov, but you did not tell me that your own flesh and blood were so talented too. You must be very proud of your daughter."

Count Orlov looked taken aback for a moment.

"My daughter," Count Orlov replied, "is but a child. Stubborn, impetuous and wilful."

Then he raised his eyes and he looked straight at Anna with an expression on his face that she had never seen before.

"It is my Orlov blood that makes my daughter so." The Count smiled. "She has achieved tremendous things with her stallion, Drakon. And I could not be any prouder of her."

At that moment the waiters swept in bearing platters of caviar and *blini* for the *entrée* and Count

Orlov was distracted by the need to resume giving orders to his staff. A hubbub of conversation struck up along with the clatter of knives and forks. In this busy atmosphere, surrounded by the buzz of the other diners, Empress Catherine focused her attention on Anna.

"I have been at the stables this morning," she said. "Drakon really is a most impressive horse. His groom tells me that you were the one who trained him."

Anna nodded. "Your Majesty, Drakon has the most wonderful nature. Sometimes I think he is more human than horse."

The Empress nodded sagely. "Then again," she mused, "I find that some humans amongst us do not have the easiest natures…" The Empress looked about the room. "Your brother, Ivan, is absent tonight. I have been watching him since I arrived at the palace. He seems an *ambitious* sort of boy."

"Ivan is… very different from me," Anna said tactfully. Then, letting her guard down, she admitted, "We don't really get on, Your Majesty."

"Is that so?" the Empress said. "Then perhaps

you will not be sad to hear that he departs under the auspices of the Lord Commander of my military tomorrow. A boy like Ivan, with his intellect and cunning, would be useful in my armed forces. So I am stationing him in Outer Siberia."

The very remotest reaches of the Russian realm. Anna felt her heart soar, her cheeks flush with relief.

"I hope you will not miss him too greatly. He will be gone for rather a long time," the Empress said as she gave Anna's hand an affirming squeeze.

The servants came and cleared the plates ready for the main course. Empress Catherine dabbed her mouth with a napkin, and then she turned to Anna once more. She reached out, and her dainty fingers brushed the filigree silver chain that held the black diamond at Anna's throat.

"Did I tell you that I was great friends with your mother?" the Empress said. "She gave you this diamond, didn't she? When she was not long for this world."

Anna nodded again. "Yes, Your Majesty. She said it is a family heirloom."

"Oh, it is far more than that!" Empress Catherine

smiled. "It is the Orlov Diamond! A black teardrop, one of the largest stones in the world, and immensely rare. It is very beautiful and ancient."

The Empress leant in close, whispering conspiratorially. "Guard this necklace well, Anna Orlov. Keep it close always, for it is precious beyond measure. There is much power in this gemstone. One day you too will hand it down to your daughter as your mother did to you. Who knows what gifts it may yet bestow on future generations."

***

That night, Anna sat at her bedroom window, peering outside at the snowy realm beyond the glass, unable to sleep. Igor had no such problems and was snoring gently at her feet. She had come back from dinner to find the hound looking rather pleased with himself. Anna's brother never turned up for dinner that evening. Katia told Anna later that the young Count Orlov had been feeling unwell and had gone straight to his room to pack. He would be leaving for Siberia first thing in the morning.

Anna put her face up so that her nose was pressed to the cold pane of the glass, and thought about the Empress's words. Against the inky blackness, she saw the moonbeams shimmering off the snow, and then in the pale light a shadow was cast, a slinking shape moving swiftly across the snowy lawn. For a moment she caught a glimpse of something, a blur of black and orange, a shock of brilliant stripes against the pure white.

"*Boris?*" As Anna spoke his name, her breath frosted the glass, turning it misty and opaque. By the time she had wiped it clean again, her tiger was gone.

"Farewell, *Borenka*," Anna said softly. She reached forward to press a kiss to the glass, a last goodbye to her beloved protector.

And when the dawn came and thawed the frost on the windows, the shape of Anna's heartfelt love remained, sparkling like a diamond in the snowy morning light.

Epilogue

My name is Anna Orlov and this has been my story. It is also inspired by the true story of Russia's greatest horse breed, the Orlov Trotter.

My father, Count Orlov, is famed for creating nearly 70 different breeds of animal, including Igor, my beloved borzoi wolfhound. However, it is for his horses that he became best known. When my father paid 60,000 roubles for the mighty foundation sire, Smetanka, it was the talk of the royal court! His men really did journey Smetanka overland from Turkey, taking almost a year to bring the horse home to the Khrenovsky estate. Smetanka's reign at the palace stables was short-lived as the winter cold of

Russia proved too brutal for his hot blood. Yet thanks to Smetanka, this one remarkable stallion, my father founded the Orlov line. Under the rule of the great Empress Catherine, Count Orlov's Trotters became a favourite of the Russian nobility, renowned for their surefootedness over the black ice of the rivers in Moscow and St Petersburg.

My father was infamous too, in much darker ways. He was a self-confessed murderer, having killed Peter the Third so that Catherine could take the throne. They say it was for this brutal act of loyalty that Her Majesty rewarded my father with our estate. You have heard my descriptions of him and I am not exaggerating when I say my father was a giant of a man, with a hideous scar disfiguring his cheek that earned him his name: *Le Balafre*. He was often away at war, fighting as the Empress's Lord Commander of the Black Sea, but whenever he came home again I lived in his dark shadow. Being a girl, I always thought he considered me lesser than my brother, Ivan. In the end though it was my ability with horses and my love for the animals that bonded us. When my father died it had been expected that Ivan, as the man of the house, would be bequeathed the Khrenovsky estate. Instead, it was I who took control. Over the years that followed, with the help of the groom, Vasily Shishkin, I established a breeding programme so that today the bloodlines of the Orlov Trotter continue. These horses are my legacy.

Anyone who owns an Orlov will tell you that they are not like other horses. They possess both a remarkable inner courage and a superior intellect. Many of their traits are almost human. The greatest of their gifts is loyalty. Such a one was the famous pink Orlov that you know as Sasha, inspired by the real-life horse, Balagur.

Like Sasha in this book, Balagur was an abused circus horse, and after that a police horse too! With his talented young dressage rider, Alexandra Korelova, and their coach George Theodorescu, this unlikely combination took on the elite world of international dressage. "I was embarrassed," Alexandra admitted, "because nobody took part at the dressage riding shows on Orlov Trotters!"

This young Russian girl and her pink Orlov defied everything the dressage world had ever known.

The pink Orlov, Balagur, was the only horse at the European Games to earn a perfect ten for his piaffe. He won his first medal at the Olympic Games in 2004 and then competed again at the Games in 2008. His fans became so devoted they followed him around the world.

I hope with all my heart that Balagur is not the last great Orlov. However, the breed is now very rare, even in Russia. You will still see them though, sometimes even performing in Moscow circuses. You will know them when you see them because they are unmistakeable, with their long legs and elongated bodies – they really do have an extra rib compared to other horses. It is the head though that really marks the Orlov as special, the narrow muzzle and flared nostrils and the broad slab of a jaw that makes them resemble a dragon. To my mind, there is no other horse in the world quite so strange or so beautiful.

As for the Orlov Diamond: in actual fact there are two of them. The White Orlov can be viewed in the Kremlin in Moscow, where it is set in the jewelled sceptre of Catherine the Great. The Black Orlov, my diamond, was believed to carry a curse that brought death to whomever possessed it – but as you now know, it meant something very different to me. It was last seen on display at the UK's Natural History Museum in 2005.